Stories *for the*

Starving Romantic

Stories *for the*

Starving Romantic

by T. J. Moran

Carmel, California
May 2017

This is a work of fiction, a compilation of stories that the author thought would be good reading, particularly at bedtime but really any time. Certainly better that reading mysteries or thrillers that might impinge on one's peace of mind. And much better than watching television. There is no connection to any people, alive or otherwise, except as specifically stated.

Stories for the
Starving Romantic

Published by SetonPublishing.com.

ISBN-13: 978-0-9989605-1-7

Printed in the United States of America

Table of Contents

Publisher's Note

I recall meeting T. J. Moran at my first attendance of the Diogenes Club of Carmel-by-the-Sea. The Diogenes Club is one of some 200 Sherlock Holmes societies around the world.

Over the years, T. J. and I became friends. I met and adored his wife, Lydia, as every man must, and wrote them into a couple of humorous Sherlockian presentations I penned and produced to entertain our fellow Sherlockians.

T. J. later became my cardiologist. Three years ago, I wrote a profile of him for a local weekly paper was focused principally on his pioneering work in heart health. (That profile is reprinted at the end of this book.)

In all the years we have known each other, and all too infrequently socialized, never did he mention that he was also a writer. Then last month, I ran into T. J. and Lydia and T. J.'s sister and brother-in-law, at the Cypress Inn, a favorite haunt, and the subject of writing and my publishing came up. That's when he told me of this book.

I must insist that he shouldn't quit his day job, but only because too many lives depend on him. But he certainly should be highly successful pursuing this avocation. His stories are well told, and, for the valued purpose for which as he designed them, they are perfect bedtime reading. I'm looking forward to reading his next volume of stories.

Tony Seton

Stories for the Starving Romantic

Author's Note

I realized sometime back that I was a "starving romantic." As a cardiologist, I bumped up against enough real life during the day that I didn't need to read about it at night. So my usual reading selections were novels of action and suspense, basically escape-from-reality type literature. Yet something was missing. I found myself searching for moments more uplifting than bullets or brawn could provide. I wanted hints of romance, or interactions between the characters that made me laugh, or touched my heart, or caused me to clinch my fist and mentally yell "Yes!" I wanted to set my book down with a smile, or a renewed belief that there was a more forgiving, loving world out there than was portrayed on the evening news. And so "Stories for the Starving Romantic" was born.

I hope that when life is pressing you down, these tales may be a lifesaver to buoy you up.

I have many people to thank for getting me to this point in my writing life, more than I could ever mention, so I will just hit the major ones.

The first is Madeline DiMaggio of whom I can't say enough. She is a mentor, writing instructor, cheerleader, and all around great friend. Being around her is like sticking your creative finger into a light socket. Your writing battery goes on overflow. Her writing classes were filled with wonderful, ingenious people that breathed life into my nearly-stillborn creations.

Hugo Gerstl is another individual *extraordinaire*. Every writer needs someone like Hugo. He was always available to read anything I wrote, made great suggestions, gave nothing but encouragement, and continued to push me to publish. While at the same time, quietly wrote more than eight fascinating books.

And my favorite editor. Amidst groans of I'm too busy, I am not going to read that again, that whole page sucks, and find someone else to edit this, my wife Lydia did an outstanding job of changing my tangle of weedy words into a garden of delight.

Finally, huge thanks to Tony Seton, a creative dynamo and published writer, who helped put all this together. The mimosas at Terry 's Lounge (in the Cypress Inn) will always be on me.

T J Moran

Carmel, California

Miracle in Manhattan

It was late one Saturday afternoon in a knee-knocking, breath-freezing February, one of the worst winters the East Coast had ever experienced. I'd just finished three hours of hearing confessions at St. Patrick's Cathedral, and as was my habit, I walked the six blocks up Fifth Avenue to the Plaza Hotel to reward myself with a glass of whisky in the Oak Room Bar.

I was surprised to find the bar packed, and then I remembered it was Winter Carnival in Central Park. This layer-wrapped crowd was spillover from the festival.

The Lord was with me, though, for I saw an empty seat at the bar. Moving closer, I noticed a long black coat draped over the back of the bar stool.

"Is this seat taken?" I asked the people on either side.

A grey haired, fashionably dressed, woman to the left, staring intently at her cell phone, replied without looking up. "I'm saving it for a friend."

Glancing around, I saw there was absolutely no other place to sit, and or even room to stand.

"Could I use it until your friend arrives?" I asked politely.

Still focused on her cell phone, she scooped up the coat and set it in her lap. As I settled onto the seat, the bartender came over. "What'll you have, Father?"

"Black Label, neat," I replied.

Hearing the bartender, the woman glanced over at me. "Oh, Father, I didn't mean to be so abrupt." Nodding at her cell phone, she said, "It's just been such a crazy day, and nothing seems to be going right."

"I've had days like that," I replied.

She glanced back at her cell phone, checked the screen, and then slowly shook her head. "It's all falling apart, and I can't seem to prevent it."

She turned toward me and her face had such anguish that I knew I couldn't ignore her implied plea. "The Chinese have a saying," I said, "'A load is much lighter when shared by two'."

She looked at me closely and then replied, "Thank you, Father." She paused. "Please understand that I don't believe in God anymore, but I desperately need someone to talk to who won't be rushing to the nearest gossip columnist." She looked at me for confirmation as she took a large sip of wine.

"I will treat this as if heard in the confessional," I assured her.

This seemed to satisfy her, because after a moment she told me the source of her angst. "The person I am waiting for is Anna Carlton, and I'm very worried about her. She's making a huge mistake, and I can't convince her otherwise."

Even in my secluded life, Anna Carlton's name was known. In fact, one would be hard pressed to find a man in America that didn't recognize her name. She had the type of pretty looks that only needed one name, hence the tabloids simply called her "Anna." Her magazine and TV coverage nearly rivaled the president's, while her dating line-up was a who's who of the rich and famous.

"My name is Jacqueline Carter and I work for the Ford Model Agency. Ten years ago, I discovered Anna in a one stop-sign town in Montana. She was a shy, naive, seventeen year old tomboy when I brought her to New York. I taught her everything she needed to know to become a top model. From elegant style and refined conversation, to how to fit into a size two without killing herself, but most importantly how to survive in this shark infested city. Over the years, she has become the daughter I never had."

I nodded.

"About two months ago she called me. She sounded terrible."

"Oh, my God, Jacqueline. This can't be happening!"

"Anna, what's wrong?"

"My face. It's bright red. I look like a cherry except this cherry is covered with blisters and sores!"

"Good Lord. Have you been to a doctor?"

"The best dermatologist in the city. I just got back."

"And?"

"He says it's an allergic reaction. But that's not the worst part." She hesitated. "He thinks it may be an allergy to my own make-up line!"

It took a moment for Jacqueline to take in the news, and then she was only able to mutter, "Oh, crap."

"No kidding. And if the press gets hold of this," Anna said, her voice rising, "my makeup line is toast."

"Now don't panic."

"Don't panic?" Anna screamed. "I look like a burn victim." She took a deep breath and slowly exhaled. "The doctor told me that I can't put anything on my face except the steroid ointment he prescribed."

"So take the steroid cream, stay out of the public eye for a few days, and everything will be fine."

"A few days?" her voice resonant with panic. "No, he said this could last as long as a month."

More silence passed, as if time was going to help, and then Jacqueline spoke, "We need to get you out of town before anyone sees you or worse yet, gets a picture of you. The press would have a feeding frenzy."

"I've racked my brain but I can't think of anywhere to go?" She moaned, "Oh, God, I can't believe this."

"Anna, we'll work this out. Give me a second to think." It was almost a full minute before Jacqueline spoke again. "I know a place you can go and sit this out. My sister's family has a cabin in upstate New York they rarely use. It's in a small town called Dignity. In the winter, the only access is by ferry. The place is so secluded that you may not see anyone, and, if you do, hopefully they won't recognize you."

"Jacqueline, even you wouldn't recognize me."

I took a sip of my drink. "I can see how this would be a concern," I ventured, not really sure where this tale was going.

"A concern?" Jacqueline laughed, and not with humor. "For a woman whose whole business, her whole life, is built on her looks, this was catastrophic!" She gestured to the bartender for a refill and then went back to her story. "The doctor had told her that until the reaction cleared up, there could be no makeup, no dying her hair, no contact lens, and no getting in the sun without covering up."

"I still don't see…"

"Father, let me give you some insight into Anna's life, then maybe you will get an idea of the extent of her problem. She came from the wide open spaces to one of the largest, most glamorous metropolises in the world. Almost overnight, she went from nowhere to notoriety, and captured the imagination of this city. Now, anything she does, anywhere she goes, it is news. She has a driver. She has a live-in cook, and a full time assistant to manage her schedule. Her trainer/masseuse and her makeup/hair stylist come by each day. Basically, everything is done for her. Now suddenly, she has to disappear without her support team for fear that one of them might inadvertently leak this to the press." Jacqueline's expression changed and she shook her head. "I love her like my own, but she is a pampered, spoiled child." After a quick glance at her watch, she continued with her story.

Anna stood on the bow of the nearly empty ferry. It was making its last trip up river for the night. A three-story boat, there were cars on the bottom level, passenger seats on the second level, and the pilot house on top. The town of Dignity was twenty miles up the river, and just one of many of the ferry's stops. Under the cover of darkness, Anna felt comfortable getting out of her car. Examining the banks of the river, she saw nothing except the dark silhouettes of the forest rising up from the dimly lit, snow covered ground. The only sound was the throb of the ferries' diesel engines.

"Beautiful night isn't it?" a male voice said.

Anna jumped.

"Sorry, didn't mean to startle you."

She half turned, all the while keeping her face out of the shine of the deck lights. The man was tall; his face obscured by shadow, except for the gleam of white teeth set in a broad smile. He wore a dark suit with a thick overcoat.

"It's been two weeks since I've been home," he continued. "The smells, the sounds, the nighttime sky - I forgot how much I missed them."

Shaking her head, Anna said, "I'm sorry but I'd like to enjoy the night alone," and swung away from him. How typical, she thought. Even on the deck of a ferry going to no-where-ville, some guy tries to pick me up. Then she realized what a prize she must look like, bundled up in three layers of clothes, knit cap pulled low over her face, and black rimmed glasses covering the rest. Maybe I was too short with him, she thought, but when she turned back to apologize, he had disappeared into the darkness.

Returning to her car, she switched on the dome light and examined her face. God, what a mess. When I get to Dignity, she affirmed, I'll drive to the house and stay there until this clears up. Looking into her back seat, she noted the pile of books, DVDs, computer, and Nutrisystem meals. Everything I need to hibernate for a month, she reminded herself.

Anna's car was the first off the ferry. A glimpse of Digniy in the dark was enough to re-enforce her plans to stay home alone indoors. The town had no more than twenty buildings whose worn exteriors were partially revealed by the light of several neon signs. The only place that appeared to be open was the Antler's Bar and Grill which was accessorized by several mud-splattered pickups parked in its lot.

She stopped at the other end of Dignity to recheck the directions that Jacqueline had given her, and then with a confidence borne of growing up in snow country, she drove on. The snow berm was piled high on either side of the roadway suggesting recent snowfall. Four miles outside of town, she made a right turn, and headed up a narrow roadway. She saw nothing but trees, and snow piled on the shoulders of the road. With the radio turned up and the car heater pumping, she sailed through the darkened forest thinking about her upcoming clothing show in two months. By then, she told herself with a deep sigh, all this will be behind me.

Approaching a sharp bend in the road, she turned the steering wheel, but the car didn't respond. Alarmed, she turned the wheel harder, but the car slid straight forward, and then WHACK! went head on into a snow bank.

The collision was soft, not the jolt she had expected. Once her hands stopped shaking, she put the car in reverse. The wheels spun, but the car remained wedged in the snowbank. She opened the door and was immediately assaulted by the cold. She hadn't realized how much the temperature had dropped. She closed the door and took a moment to gather her thoughts. Glancing around, there were no lights and no homes visible. Not to worry, she told herself. If I can handle New York City, I can manage this. She took out her cell phone. No bars.

"Typical," she said, dropping the phone into her purse. She glanced around. "Okay, I'll just walk back into town and get help." Speaking out loud seemed to ease the loneliness of the situation.

Swinging the door open again, she stepped out. Once again, the cold struck her. With her fourth step, her foot slipped and she went down on her butt.

"Damn," she moaned. She rolled over, got to her knees, and stood up. One step and -plop- she was on her backside again.

Maybe this walking to town isn't such a good idea, she thought as the cold burrowed under her coat.

She was crawling toward her car when she heard music, and then suddenly she was in the full glare of someone's headlights. Still on her knees, she lifted her arm and waved. The vehicle, apparently a truck, pulled to a stop, its lights still blinding her. She heard the truck's door open and Bob Seger's "Night Moves" filled the night. The music stopped abruptly, and then she heard someone's footsteps approaching.

Shading her eyes with one hand, she said, "I could use some

help, please."

There was a pause, then a male voice said softly, "I'm sorry but I'd like to enjoy the night alone."

Her supporting hand slipped and she went face first onto the ice. In the distance, she heard a muffled laugh. She didn't see anything funny. Men didn't treat her like this. Still flat on the road, she glared in his direction, "If you are looking for an apology, forget it," she said tersely.

The night was quiet, and then she heard footsteps moving away and the truck door slam. The vehicle backed up and started to go around her.

She couldn't believe it. He was just going to leave her. "Wait! Wait! Don't go!"

The truck stopped and she heard a window go down. "Did you say something?"

She took a deep breath. "I'm sorry I was ... rude," she managed in a somewhat plaintive tone. "Now can you help me?"

"Well, that was so heartfelt that how can I resist?" He backed the truck up and got out.

"You are in the middle of a pool of black ice," he said. "It builds up here every winter. The only people that slip here are tourists." He paused. "So I guess you aren't from around here?"

He cautiously stepped out on the ice, walked over, and put a hand down for her. He was pulling her up when - whoosh - he slipped and landed hard on top of her. There was a moment before either of them spoke, then Anna said, "So I guess you aren't from around here either."

He started laughing, and it was so infectious, so honest, that she had to smile. Moving carefully, he slid off of her and sat up.

"Let's start over." He put out his hand. "I'm Jake Mather."

"Anna, eh, Anna... Smith," Anna replied as they shook hands.

"Well, Ms. Smith, let's get your car out of that snowbank." He leaned back and stared up at a sky that would make a planetarium drool.

"Not to be repetitive, but it is a beautiful night."

With great care, Jake carefully helped her into her car. He attached a tow rope from his truck to her vehicle, and within a few minutes had her back on the road. Climbing out, he walked over to her window.

"Where are you headed?"

"1010 Wilderness Road."

He nodded. "The Winsor place. Nice digs. I'll follow to make sure you get there safely."

"Oh, no," Anna said automatically, thinking he'll want to come in, have a drink, and I'll never get rid of him. "That won't be necessary."

He swept his arm toward the hole her car had made in the snow bank. "And if that happens again?"

"Didn't think of that." she said. "Yes, I'd appreciate the company. And once more, thank you."

The rest of the drive was uneventful. Anna did feel protected with him behind her, but again wondered what she would do if he wanted to stay. When she finally turned into the plowed driveway of 1010, she heard him honk and then his truck continued on down the road.

She was relieved that there was no uncomfortable scene at the front door, yet oddly disappointed that a man could so easily resist her charms. Opening her car door, the interior light went on and she saw herself in the rearview mirror. It was a return to reality.

"What the hell was I thinking," she said. "With this face, I'd have needed a gun to get him inside."

The home was nice. Three bedrooms, two baths, two fireplaces, a huge modern kitchen, hot tub, and forced air heating. It was minimally decorated with no clutter, just a couple of deep couches, a few paintings on the walls, and some tasteful lamps. Actually, it was so impersonal that Anna figured it was more of a rental than a home.

Unloading her car, she put her packaged meals in the kitchen, and took everything else upstairs. In the bathroom light, she once again cursed her ruined face with its bright red, blistered skin. She knew it was only temporary, but it was so embarrassing, so degrading. Always she had been the center of her universe when it came to looks. High school homecoming queen four years in a row. A New York fashion model with instant success. Her beauty had opened every door, from the Ford Model Agency to Donald Trump's Christmas party. Now it was gone and even though the loss was not permanent, it was the anchor of who she was, and how she interacted with the rest of the world.

She unpacked and put on her pajamas. After brushing her teeth, she rubbed on the steroid cream.

What a day, she thought. At least now I can finally relax. Taking a sleeping pill, she climbed into the king-size bed, put her sleeping mask on, and was almost instantly in the arms of Morpheus.

The first sensation she noticed when she awakened was the cold. Deep, bone chilling cold that struck her even under the bedcovers. Removing her mask, she looked out the window and saw that a new day had dawned. But why was it so cold? She went to the bathroom and hit the light switch and got her answer. Nothing happened.

Bundling up, she went downstairs. Outside it was snowing heavily. There was already at least a foot of new snow on her car roof. In the kitchen, she picked up the phone to find out when she could expect the return of her electric power. The portable phone battery was dead. Checking, she found her cell phone still had no bars.

"No, problem. A little fire in the fireplace and this place will be toasty." Rubbing her arms to get the chill off, she moved into the living room. There was no wood by the fireplace.

"Okay," she said resolutely, "I'll get dressed, drive into town, and wait there until the electricity is back on."

No power meant no hot water, so no shower. Shaking the entire time, she yanked on three layers of the heaviest clothes she had brought. With her knit cap pulled down tight and three wool scarves wound around her neck, she headed to the front door.

Outside, it quickly became apparent that she wasn't going to use her car. A snow plow had come by during the night and now there was a frozen pile of snow in the driveway blocking access to the street. And if that wasn't enough, the roadway was covered with a foot of new snow.

Defeated, she retreated into the house. As the afternoon wore on, she got colder, hungrier, and more distressed. There was no microwave, no TV, and no radio.

It continued to snow until she could hardly see her car.

I can't go through the night like this, she decided. It's time to find some help before the afternoon gets any later. There must be someone living around here who is better prepared for winter than this place.

Adding a fourth layer of clothes, she passed the front hall mirror on her way out. She grimaced; any attempt at fashion had been abandoned.

Since she had seen no sign of life driving out to her house the night before, she started walking in the opposite direction. After two miles, she started to worry since all she had seen were deserted homes, but then she noticed a light in the front window of a small log cabin. There was an ancient truck in the driveway and a rusty swing set in the front yard.

She shuffled through the snow up to the front door and knocked. No answer. She knocked again, and then pounded. Still no answer. Peaking in the window, she saw the archetypical mountain cabin - bright Indian throw rugs on worn hardwood floors, plaid and leather furniture, snowshoes and wood skis mounted on the walls, and best of all, dancing flames in a stone hearth.

What should she do? She was freezing while on the other side of this door, there was warmth. It was a no-brainer decision. She turned the doorknob and pushed. The heavy wooden door opened for her.

"Hello? Anyone home?" The house was silent.

Closing the door, she moved toward the warmth of the fire. She heard a growling noise behind her and turned. A huge dog with a mouthful of jagged teeth raced at her from an open doorway. She raised her arms, lurching backwards in defense. The dog leapt up, putting his front paws on her chest, and knocked her down. She struck her head on the floor and everything went dark.

Gradually, she became aware of a crushing sensation on her chest. Eyes still closed, she tried to push it off. The same growling brought her quickly alert. She found herself flat on a couch with the huge beast that had attacked her making himself comfortable on her chest. Cautiously, she tried to ease him off. He responded with bared teeth and a growl. Closing her eyes, she put her hands protectively over her face.

"Get off her, you oaf!" a man shouted, and the weight disappeared.

Opening her eyes, she found a tall, black-haired man with azure colored eyes staring down at her. His firm, angular face was softened by a wide smile. With his well-worn Levis, Pendleton shirt, and dark brown snow boots, he could have been an ad for an adventure magazine.

"Well," he said, "three times in less than twenty-four hours."

Hearing his voice, she realized this was Jake Mather. And just as suddenly, she pictured her own appearance. She reached up to pull her cap down and found it was gone. So were her scarves and jacket.

"You got a pretty nasty blow to the head with that fall," he said, "You should take everything slow and easy."

Sitting up, she felt dizzy and slowly leaned back against the couch.

"Sorry about Yukon here. He gets a little too friendly when he sees someone new, especially a woman. I keep telling him not to jump up on people."

"But he almost bit me a moment ago."

Jake gestured to the couch. "He thought you were trying to push him off. He considers this couch his. But it's all a bluff. He'd never bite you."

Lifting her hand, Anna found a tender, swollen area on the back of her skull. The dizziness was receding, only to be replaced by a mild headache.

"Again, I'm sorry about Yukon." He paused for a moment. "Can I get you something? A cup of tea, glass of water, whatever?"

"A couple of Advil's with tea would be nice."

She heard him puttering in the kitchen, and then he was back with the tea and the pills. As she swallowed them down, he said, "Not to be un-neighborly, but how is it that you ended up on the floor of my house?"

Anna set the glass down and ran her fingers through her hair, trying to get some semblance of order in the tangles. "The storm knocked the electricity out in my rental house. I finally decided that with no heat, no food, and no hot water, I was going to have trouble making it through the night."

He nodded, "Well, you are more than welcome to stay as long as you need." He added. "I guess this isn't the vacation you had intended."

"Other than the freezing, filthy, starving part, it's just what the doctor ordered."

"The doctor?"

She ran her hand over her face. "I had an allergic reaction."

"I wasn't going to ask." He smiled at her. "Even so, you have a nice, friendly face."

Friendly face? Oh, how the mighty have fallen, she thought.

Yukon came over and laid his head on her lap and looked up at her. Cautiously, she stretched her hand out and stroked his head. He climbed up on the couch and leaned against her.

"Looks like you made a friend." Jake gestured toward a far door. "You mentioned filthy and hungry. If you feel up to it, you are welcome to use my shower" he said, gesturing toward a far door. "And while you're cleaning up, I can fix something to quell that hunger."

"How is it that you have hot water and electricity?"

"A generator and a gas water heater."

The hot water felt like a caress from heaven. The view in the mirror afterwards looked like a vision from hell. Her dark roots were becoming more obvious, and her blistered, red face even puffier. All this, combined with her thick black rimmed glasses, solidified the picture of a fashion-less, frump.

Leaving the bathroom, she passed through the master bed room and her curiosity took over as she noticed a half-dozen framed photographs on his bureau. She moved from photograph to photograph. Jake in winter garb standing next to Yukon holding a trophy. A beautiful woman with her arm possessively around Jake, both of them smiling fiercely. An older couple dressed casually, standing by a river, their facial features identifying them as Jake's parents.

"Hey, in there. The food's ready. And the chef doesn't like to be kept waiting."

On a bookshelf in the corner, she saw a row of trophies. Before she could move to examine them, Yukon trotted into the room. He gently grabbed her arm in his mouth, and pulled her toward the door.

She hadn't realized how hungry she was until she saw the food.

Jake stood at the table, his arms spread wide. "The specialty of the house - a Mexican omelet with homemade salsa."

Anna was half way through the omelet before she let the taste really seep in. "This is delicious." She smiled at him then glanced around. "Where's your wife?"

He raised his eyebrows.

"I saw the picture and the ring on her finger," she said nodding toward the bedroom.

It was a moment before he spoke. "We're divorced. I keep the picture because it's a good shot of Yukon." He reached down to pet the dog. "So, how about you? Where are you from?"

"New York City." She paused. "And a bit lost in all this snow and wilderness."

"Yeah, it took me a while to adjust when I moved here from the city."

"You lived in New York?"

"Ages ago."

Anna glanced around the cabin. "Privacy can be nice," she said, "but this just is a little too private for me."

He laughed. "It grows on you."

"Along with the moss." She chuckled and took another bite of her omelet. "It still must get lonely."

"Some of the loneliest times of my life occurred in New York City. What I finally came to realize is that loneliness is not a location; it's a state of mind. But you're right, at first I did have trouble adjusting." He pointed at her empty plate. "Now that you've finished, I'll show you my antidote for loneliness."

He led her through the small kitchen and out the backdoor.

Immediately a chorus of howls shattered the stillness of the evening. Anna jumped back. There must have been twenty small dog houses in the area behind the house, all nearly covered with snow. And chained to each one was an excited, barking dog.

"Oh, my God. Is this a dog pound or something?"

He smiled at her questioning look. "This is my cure. These are sled dogs. I race them."

He stepped from the porch into the yard, and the noise level rose even higher. Pointing to each of the dogs, he called out their names. "Lightening. Blizzard. Avalanche. Stormy. Hurricane. Tornado. Flood." The rest of the names were lost in the cries of the dogs.

"Such cuddly names," Anna said, looking around the yard. "Not to be rude, but these dogs look like refuges from the ASPCA. I thought sled dogs were pure bred huskies or malamutes?"

"Believe it or not, these are huskies, not the show type, but rather a mix that's been bred for speed and endurance. Malamutes are beautiful, but too slow for racing." He gestured to the dog yard. "And, yes, to the inexperienced eye, they do look like riffraff." He noticed her shivering, and gestured to the house. "Hey, let's get you back to some warmth."

Settling in front of the fire with another cup of tea, Anna said, "So what do you do up here when you are not rescuing obnoxious female tourists?"

"I'm a doctor."

"There's enough business around here?"

"Once the snow melts, the population jumps up pretty quickly."

Anna grinned. "That's probably the only thing that does jump around here."

Jake smiled. "Oh, you'd be surprised at all the action in this town."

"Really?" Anna tilted her head. "Like what?"

"Well… for example, karaoke night at the Antler's Bar."

"A must?"

"Epic!" He chuckled. "Just one of the options on the Dignity entertainment list."

Anna laughed. "I'm betting that's a very short list." She took a sip of tea. "So what brought you here… other than the karaoke?"

"I was born here."

"Somehow I got the impression that you were from New York City."

"I did four years of college and all my medical training there. In fact, I even had a medical practice there for several years." His stare moved from her to the fireplace, and his smile slipped away.

"Why'd you return?"

"A moment of clarity." He stood up and jabbed the fire with a metal poker, causing the flames to spark up. "I realized I wasn't meant to be a city dweller."

"And what brought you to that decision?"

His answer was interrupted by the ring of a phone. "Excuse me," Jake said and moved over to the table to picked it up. "Hello. Oh, hi Jennie. How are you doing?" A pause. "I'll be right there, don't worry." He hung the phone up, and turned to Anna who was just finishing her tea. "That was a patient of mine. Needs me to come over right away." He gestured at the fireplace. "Feel free to stay and enjoy the cabin. I'll be back shortly, probably." He started turning away and then stopped. "Why don't you come with me? I'm taking the dog sled."

Anna nearly choked on the tea. "You're kidding, right?"

"When are you ever going to get another chance to ride in a dog sled?"

Anna shook her head. "It's not happening."

"Do you have some other place you need to be? Like a freezing home with no electricity?" He reached down and pulled her out of her chair. "I guarantee that you won't be cold, and the ride will be electric."

She threw up her arms. "All right, if you promise to take it slow."

In ten minutes, he had six dogs harnessed, cushions in the sled basket, and a heavy ski parka for her. He helped her climb in, and covered her with a heavy woolen blanket. Lastly, he tucked a rifle down into the basket next to her.

Anna had grown up around rifles but was still a bit surprised.

"We need a rifle for this?"

"Just routine. Don't worry. So are you ready?"

She had barely nodded when he pulled the tie rope free and yelled, "HIKE!"

The transition was sudden. One moment, they were stationary, the next they were flying down the snow-covered driveway next to the cabin. With a sweeping, sliding turn, barely missing the truck, they headed up the street, sailing over the soft white blanket of snow on the road.

Anna's initial apprehension was quickly replaced by near hysteria, as they charged through the street seemingly with no control over the sled. Gradually, her anxiety fell away, and changed to excitement. On either side, the dim outlines of trees raced by, with the only sound that of the sled runners slicing through the snow. The dogs were silent, doing what they loved, running on this endless path of white, with the sounds of their footsteps muffled by the snow.

Yukon and another dog were harnessed as lead dogs, both with red lights attached to the leather straps on their backs.

Jack wore a bright head lamp helping to light the way. He switched if off and leaned down next to Anna. "Look up," he said.

The sky was like the black, velvet cloth a jeweler will use as background to accentuate the brilliance of a diamond, only this cloth held an unbelievable array of gleaming stars that needed nothing to accentuate their beauty. She couldn't remember the last time she had looked up into such a night sky. A moment of regret passed as she realized that the last time may have been when she had lived in Montana. Had she lost so much of herself to the city, she wondered, that she let such beauty slip so easily out of her life?

Dangling her hand out of the sled, she scooped up some fallen snow and brought it to her lips. Yes, it had the same fresh, invigorating taste she remembered as a child when she played in the snow with her brother. Leaning back in the sled basket, she closed her eyes, relishing the simple thrill of floating through the darkness, surrounded by silence. She couldn't remember the last time she had felt so relaxed. It was as if she could sense what peace tasted like.

Thoughts of Montana emerged - memories of snuggling against her dad on the hard, metal tractor seat as he drove home from a day in the wheat fields, the endless sky that filled with pinks and reds in the summer evenings, their old fashioned kitchen with its enticing smells, and her mother singing in her slightly off key voice while she did the house chores. Anna had been surrounded by love, security, and a feeling of home. Yes, there had been tough times, disagreements, and growing pains, but the underlying feeling had always been one of comfort, of being where she belonged. Had she ever felt like that in New York City? No such memory came to mind. When had she become so one-dimensional, so shallow that life had become just about her looks and parties? And wasn't it time to do something about it?

"Here we are," Jake said. "WHOA!" he yelled to the team as he stepped on the thick piece of rubber attached to the sled that served as a brake.

Tying the sled to a nearby tree, he helped Anna out, and then pulled a black doctor's bag from beneath the cushions. He gestured toward the door of a small house, light beaming from the windows.

"Does everyone have electricity but me?" Anna said.

"No. Everyone has a generator but you," Jake replied.

As they approached the house, the front door flew open, revealing a near frantic man who cried, "Doc, thank God. She's in the bedroom."

"Mark, this is Anna," Jake said calmly.

Mark nodded, and then said over his shoulder as he turned back into the house, "Nice to meet you, ma'am."

They followed him down a hallway into the bedroom.

A young woman, her hair matted with sweat, was propped up by pillows against the headboard. She was very pregnant.

"I think it's time, Dr. Jake."

"How often are the contractions, Jennie?"

"Every one to two minutes, and getting real strong."

"Oh, my God, she's having a baby," Anna whispered, or at least she thought she'd whispered until she realized that everyone in the room was looking at her.

Jake smiled and turned to the husband. "Mark, everything is going to be fine, but I'm going to need your help."

"My help?" he croaked in disbelief. "Doc, I don't have any experience with something like this." He looked down at the floor, "And I tend to faint at the sight of blood."

"Mark, it's no big deal. I'll walk you through everything."

"What's your assistant going to do?" he said nodding at Anna.

Anna found herself again the focus of the room. Jake put his hand on Mark's shoulder. "I'm afraid she's not…"

Anna cut him off. "I'm ready whenever you are, doctor?"

Jake spun around.

"Shall we get started?" Anna said with a shrug of her shoulders.

Jake paused and then faced Mark. "Bring me a pan of very hot water while my… assistant… helps me prepare Jennie."

With a sigh of relief, Mark charged out of the room.

Jake asked softly, "Are you sure about this?"

"I played a nurse on TV once," she said with a serious look on her face, which she turned into a smile. "And, I've seen lots of babies born," she said, trying to keep her voice steady. As Jake turned away, she added, "Baby animals."

Before Jake could respond, Jennie let out a cry. "It's coming. It's coming."

Jacqueline paused in her recital to drain the last of her wine.

I noticed that my glass was also empty. I never had more than one drink, ever. Yet before I knew what I was doing, I'd raised my hand to the bartender, "Another round for both of us, please." Somehow the need to rush back to an empty room in the rectory had gotten lost in my desire to hear the rest of this tale.

Mark had been pacing outside the bedroom, but the cry of a newborn brought him rushing into the bedroom. His first glance caught his exhausted, smiling wife in bed, holding Anna's hand. His second glance found Jake holding a squirming, glistening bundle of legs and arms.

"It's a girl," his wife said. After a moment, she added gently, "As we decided, her name is going to be Jennifer, but her middle name will be Anna." She smiled at Anna. "I never could have gotten through this without you and Dr. Jake," Jennie said. "And since it's a girl, I can't really name her Jennifer Jake."

Could Anna remember a moment as precious as this? She'd had compliments from movie heart throbs, presents from rock stars, and wooing from empire building magnates, yet nothing could compare to this simple, intimate gesture. How could she have let her "glamorous life" pull her so far away from such true emotions?

"I am so honored," she whispered, trying to keep her voice from cracking while she felt her eyes filling with tears.

Later, as Jake packed his black bag in the sled, he looked at Anna. "You were great. In fact, you did so well that I think a drink at the Antler's bar is indicated. It's just a short ride down the road."

"Jake, I can't…"

He held up his hands halting her reply. "Now I know this offer has taken your breath away, but it's the least I can do to pay back my new assistant."

"I'm too embarrassed to go out in public with this face."

"Nonsense. You look fine." He paused. "How about if I promise a secluded, dark corner near the fireplace?"

"And we don't do karaoke!"

In what seemed like just minutes, they were pulling up into the plowed parking lot of the Antler's battered building.

Their entrance was met with a chorus of congratulations and job-well-done's by the twenty or so patrons that were crowded inside. A path opened up as they walked to the bar. A barrel of a man with a long, grey streaked beard, and a NY Yankee cap, stood behind the bar smiling at them. He looked at Jake. "Mark Jacobs called. Gave us the good news. Said if you showed up, all your drinks were on him." He glanced at Anna. "You must be the new assistant he mentioned." His smile got broader as he lifted his ball cap. "Nice to meet you, ma'am. About time Jake got some companionship, eh, I mean an assistant." He winked at Anna, and added "His usual date here has four legs. And speaking of that date, where is Yukon?"

"I left him outside," Jake replied. "And don't you have some drinks to mix?"

The next few hours were a whirlwind of drinks, toasts, and

honest laughter. Jake and his friends pulled Anna in with their welcoming camaraderie. It was fun watching Jake among his friends, spreading humor, compassion, and intelligence - whatever the moment called for.

At one point, Anna went into the bathroom. When she was leaving, she paused to check her makeup. For a moment, she didn't recognize the red, blistered face in the mirror. At first she was horrified, and then she realized that no one else in the bar seemed to care. The bad lighting and the heavy drinking by the bar patrons had probably also saved her from being recognized. These people had accepted her as she was, not what she looked like. She couldn't remember the last time that had happened. And she couldn't explain why it felt so good.

As the night progressed, she found herself in deep conversation with an older man, the owner of the town's general store. She gradually steered the conversation to Jake.

"I've known him since he was born. Watched him grow up and move away. Watched him come back and settle here. It was our gain and New York's loss, I always said."

"Did you know his wife?" Anna asked.

"No, but me and most of the townsfolk have always wanted to thank her."

"Why's that?"

"She's the reason that Jake moved back." He took a pull on his beer. "Jake is pretty closed mouth, but one night he got a bit tipsy, as all of us do on occasion," he said with a sheepish grin, "and spilled his guts. When he met her, she was a waitress, trying to become an actress. I guess things happened pretty fast, and boom, they were married. Jake opened his medical practice and she quit her waitress job to chase her acting career." He held up his empty beer stein. "Hey, Mac, what's a guy got to do to get a refill?"

"Call your wife," Mac yelled. "She told me your limit was three. You work it out with her."

"Isn't that always the way," he said to Anna. "Your wife cuts off all your fun." He pushed his empty glass away. "It was the opposite for Jake though. His wife claimed he was cutting her fun off. She wanted to party, to be seen in all the right places, and with all the right people. Jake on the other hand was trying to start up a medical practice, and didn't have the time or the desire to party until all hours of the night. And he didn't particularly like the people she was partying with. He thought they were all phonies. If you'll pardon my French, the exact description was 'bull shit artists'."

"I've had experience with the type," Anna said.

"She started staying out later and later, until one night she didn't come home. Apparently, she met some producer from LA who was going to make her a star. She divorced Jake and moved to LA. Jake moved back here and swore off city living, or ever getting involved with another woman like that."

"What happened to her?"

"Jake told me she got some bit parts, but not in any movies I've ever heard of." He lifted his empty beer mug. "So I salute you, young lady. You're one of very few women that Jake has ever brought here, so he must think highly of you."

"Don't bet the farm on that one," she said, wondering how with her face she could even be in the running.

Jake slid up next to them. "I'm sorry to steal my assistant away, Bill, but I think it's time that we medical professionals head home."

After a long round of goodbyes, they went out to the parking lot. The dogs immediately jumped up and began to howl.

"What's wrong with them," Anna said.

"They want to run and howl at the moon," he said with a laugh, "and so do I."

Anna grabbed him by his arms and stared into this face. "Do we need a designated driver here?"

Jake laughed again. "Once I start these dogs, they'll take us straight home. All we have to do is hang on."

He staggered slightly, and Anna caught him. "Are you okay?"

"I'm fine. And if I might say so, a number of my friends in there thought you were pretty fine."

"Oh, I'm just Miss Beauty Pageant."

"If they can't see any deeper than that, I wouldn't call them my friends." He walked toward the sled. "Hey, why don't you help me drive these guys home? There's nothing to it."

It had been a night of firsts, so she said, "Why not."

He spent the next several minutes instructing her about handling the sled, the use of the brake, and most important, the commands for the dogs.

Anna put one foot on each of the runners behind the sled, and grasped the handle bar. Jake got on right behind her, reaching around with one hand to hold the bar while the other held the tie line.

"Ready?"

"As ready as I'm ever going to be."

He yanked the tie line loose, and yelled "HIKE!"

With a jerk, they took off. Caught off balance, Anna started to fall but Jake's strong embrace caught her and kept her upright.

"Doesn't look good if the driver falls off," he said chuckling. "From now on it should go pretty smoothly since we are just going to follow the road home, and there is no one out at this time of night."

Jake held her tightly between his arms as he kept both his hands on the sled handle. Leaning back against him, Anna swayed along with the sled movement. It was a warm, intimate feeling that somehow felt just right.

They twisted along the county roads, taking the same route that Anna had taken just the other night in her car. Anna was shocked when she realized all that had happened in just one day. As they passed the black ice where Anna had slid out, Jake said, "It's funny how first impressions can be so misleading."

"So I'm not still the stuck up bitch from the city?"

"Oh, that hasn't changed," he said, then issued a groan when she jabbed him with her elbow. "I meant that you no longer see me as a small town hick trying to pick you up."

"You're right," Anna said softly. "Now I see you as a dedicated doctor..."she paused and then louder, "hoping to find a date anywhere you can."

They both laughed, and it seemed to Anna that Jake's arms got a little tighter around her, or maybe it was that she leaned a little more into him.

It was a half a mile further down the road when Yukon began to bark, and then all the dogs started barking and whining.

"WHOA!" Jake yelled, bringing the sled to a stop. The dogs kept up the barking and howling.

"What's wrong?" Anna said looking around.

Jake stepped off the sled and tied the sled rope to a sapling. He began to walk forward. "Stay here," he said over his shoulder. "I'm going to..." His words were cut off as a huge shape bounded out of the darkness into the moonlight and struck him from behind. Jake was flung forward with such force that he slid up to the front of the dog team. His head lamp was knocked off, but in its glare, Anna recognized the massive shape. It was a huge bull moose.

The dogs were really howling now, all turned toward the moose, snarling and snapping. She saw Yukon pull the team around, placing himself between Jake and the moose. Jake tried to stand, only to fall back. She heard his voice, weak but firm, "Anna, get into the trees. Now!"

The moose put its head down and used its antlers to fling a dog that had come too close back into the pack.

Oh, my God, Anna thought. The dogs are tied up. They can't defend themselves.

Yukon lunged forward and sunk his teeth into the leg of the moose, only to be thrown airborne. Anna turned to go for the trees and then stopped. She was suddenly a Montana girl who had grown up hunting with her dad and brothers. The experience of those years of tracking and shooting took over. She pulled the blanket off the sled basket and found the rifle. It was the similar to the Remington she'd fired so many times. Levering a quick round into the chamber, she raised the rifle, and fired into the air, hoping to scare the animal off. The moose paused for an instant, but instead of fleeing, turned toward her and charged.

"Oh, hell, where is Anna?" Jacqueline said looking at her wrist watch and checking her cell phone for messages. "She should have been here a long time ago."

With a start, I realized I was still sitting in the Oak Room Bar, not on a back road in the wilds of upper New York State facing a raging moose. I waved at the bartender.

"Another round, Father?" he asked.

"No, but a large cup of black coffee, please." I turned to Jacqueline. "Anything for you?"

"No, I'm fine."

The bartender set the coffee down.

"I hope you're not ending the story now," I said to Jacqueline.

"Well, that's my problem. There is no end to this story, at least not the end I want."

From long years in the confessional I knew that people liked to tell their story in their own way and at their own pace, so I just nodded.

"Well, thank God for experience and especially for luck. Anna's next shot apparently hit that four-legged monster a glancing blow to the head. It didn't kill him but it drove him off. Jake, as it later turned out, had four broken ribs and a ruptured spleen. Yukon was pretty beaten up, while the other dogs had just minor bruises. Anna helped Jake into the sled basket, and at his insistence, put Yukon in his lap. With Jake's guidance, she managed to get the team back into town. By the time they reached the Antler bar, Jake was nearly unconscious. He was taken by Medivac helicopter to the nearest hospital. Anna spent the entire night nursing Yukon, and by morning he wouldn't let her leave his side. Everyone recovered nicely. Everyone but Anna."

"Anna was injured?"

"Not that you could see."

"I don't understand."

"As much as she wanted to, she couldn't allow herself to go with Jake to the hospital. In fact, she had to disappear. She knew his accident would draw news reporters from all over. Even with her rash and lack of make-up, the odds were that she would be recognized. She got someone to help her with her car, and caught the ferry out the next evening. I arranged for her to spend the rest of her recovery in a secluded location. Meanwhile, her dermatologist discovered that it wasn't her make-up she was allergic to, but rather a probiotic that she had been using. So now she's back, her make-up line is booming, and she looks great."

"So what's the trouble?"

"Oh, she won't admit it to me, but she's changed. She's become more of a homebody. Rarely goes out. Keeps talking about small town life. About getting back to her rural values. Wears her hair down and free. Uses minimal makeup except for her photo shoots." Jacqueline shook her head. "I knew that some-day it might happen, but I never thought it would be such a shock to her system."

"What might happen?"

"Love. She's head over heels for Jake."

"That's great," I said. "Does he know?"

"That's the problem. She's afraid once he knows who she really is, he's going to see her as nothing but a flashy version of his ex-wife. Maybe even worse, since at least his ex-wife didn't lie to him about who she was when they first met."

"Well, maybe he won't care?"

"She's too afraid to take that chance." Jacqueline sighed. "She can face down a charging moose, yet she's afraid to face rejec-tion. Go figure." Once again, she glanced at her watch. "Damn! Everything is going to be ruined."

"Am I missing something here?" I said.

"Anna's leaving tomorrow for Europe. It's a two week promo-tion tour for her make-up line, and then she's going to stay another three months." Jacqueline slapped the bar with her hand. "This whole thing is going to eat at her, and hiding in Europe is not the answer. So, I took things into my own hands."

"Ah."

"I checked out this Jake Mather. He appears to be a really good guy. So I figured, if they just happened to bump into each other, maybe nature would take its course."

"Bump into each other? Like where?"

"At the Winter Carnival in Central Park. He's there with his dog team. Several mushers are putting on a short sled dog race to raise money for childhood leukemia. After the race, the mushers are going to take the kids for sled rides. I figured I would get Anna to go for a walk in the park and angle her over toward the races. Hopefully, the two might meet. But now it's so late, the sled dog teams are probably gone."

I tried to gain the bartender's attention, only to realize that his attention and everyone else's was focused behind me.

"Jacqueline," a melodious voice said over my shoulder, "I'm so sorry to be late. Last minute packing can take forever."

I turned and there she was, Anna of the tabloids. She didn't have the sexy starlet look; instead she had a wholesome, girl-next-door appearance. And - Lord forgive me for these thoughts - if I'd had a girl like that next door, I would never have left home.

Jacqueline and Anna embraced as I stood up. Jacqueline introduced me, and they both invited me to stay. A nearby barstool had been vacated, so I pulled it over.

They were just starting to talk when I interrupted them. "Excuse me while I make a bathroom stop and a phone call." I pointed at Anna's and Jacqueline's coats hanging on their bar stools. "Why don't I hang these up for you at the front door?"

Anna smiled. "That would be nice, Father."

When I returned twenty minutes later, they were deep in conversation. Jacqueline turned toward me. "Oh, there you are, Father." She nodded toward Anna. "I told her that you know the whole story. She is still determined to run from her emotions. Maybe you have some advice you could offer?" She put her hand up in front of Anna, halting Anna's reply.

I paused to collect my thoughts. "Ms. Carlton, I will just say that God works in mysterious ways." Behind her I could see Jacqueline shaking her head at me. "Sometimes," I added, "we just have to let His plan play out."

Jacqueline leaned in between us. "I told you, Father, that I don't believe any of this spiritual mantra about God has a plan, and we are just supposed to leave it all up to Him."

I was about to respond when something knocked against my barstool. I looked down to find the cause and saw a huge dog nuzzling Anna's leg. She saw the dog and lovingly grabbed his head in her hands. Almost immediately, her gaze moved up to check the room.

I heard Anna's sudden intake of breath. A man straight from the North Country, in a ski-parka and knit cap, was striding toward us.

The man reached down and grabbed the dog by his collar. "Yukon? What are you doing?" He looked up at us. "I am so sorry. I'm not sure what got into my dog." He stopped in mid-apology, and stared. "Anna?"

"Jake." They stared at each other for the longest moment, and then Anna said gently, "What are you doing here?"

Jake never took his gaze off her face, "Following Yukon."

I'm not sure that either one of them heard their words since so much more was being said through their eyes.

Jacqueline seemed dumbfounded, so I broke the silence by introducing both of us. Jake reluctantly took his eyes off Anna and shook our hands.

Seeming to rally, Jacqueline spoke, "I've heard wonderful

things about you, Jake."

"Thank you," he replied with a smile, and then swung back to Anna. "What happened to you? I looked everywhere."

She hesitated, and then said, "I'm so sorry, Jake. I'm not Anna Smith. I'm Anna Carlton."

Jake's brow furrowed momentarily, and then his face flooded with recognition. He paused a moment, taking it all in, and then blurted out, "That doesn't explain why you vanished."

"I was trying to hide my identity so I lied about a lot of things. I figured once you discovered my deception, you'd think I was no different than your ex-wife, and want nothing to do with me."

Jake slowly shook his head and said softly, "If my ex-wife had helped me deliver a baby, had risked her own life to save mine, or had even enjoyed swigging beers with my friends, I would never have let her go."

Once again, conversation died as the two continued to stare at each other.

Jacqueline touched Jake's arm, breaking the spell. "How did you find us?" she asked in awe.

"It was the strangest thing," he said. "I had tied the dogs up and gone for a cup of coffee. When I came back, I found Yukon howling and straining against his rope. I thought he wanted to get into the truck, but when I untied him he took off. I chased him across the park, up the steps here of the Plaza, and into the bar." Jake shrugged his shoulders. "There was nothing I could do to stop him. He had his own plan."

I stared pointedly at Jacqueline, and repeated softly, "'His own plan'."

The hostess interrupted us and said to Jake, "Sir, I am sorry but dogs are not allowed in the bar."

Jake pivoted back and his question included all three of us. "Can we possibly take this somewhere else?"

"You two go," Jacqueline said, as she put her hand on Anna's back and gave her a little push. "Father and I have things to discuss."

I watched as Jake and Anna, now hand in hand, went out the door with Yukon trailing close behind.

When I twisted back to the bar, I noticed Jacqueline staring at her empty glass.

"Are you okay?" I asked.

"After my husband died unexpectedly several years ago, I became very bitter about religion. I blamed God and abandoned Him." She shook her head. "But you were right, Father. God does have a plan and we just need to believe in Him." She glanced over at me. "As far as I am concerned, what happened here tonight was a miracle." She pushed her empty glass away. "All of these years I have denied faith, and now I see how wrong I was." She paused, "And, you know, it makes me feel really good to have Him back into my life."

On my return to the rectory, I made a detour into the cathedral and knelt down in the front pew.

"Well, Lord, I'm happy that Jacqueline has found her way back to religion, but I don't want You upset with me. I didn't interfere with Your divine plan. I merely let Yukon smell Anna's coat in the park, then dragged it all the way back to the Oak Room Bar. Now, what's the harm in that except maybe she'll need to get the coat cleaned?"

* * * * *

Author's Note: I spent a week in northern Minnesota dog sledding and loved it, so it became a part of this story.

I also loved the Oak Room Bar in the Plaza Hotel in Manhattan which sadly is now open just for special events. That bar reeked of days gone past, of horse drawn carriages, of men in heavy overcoats with top hats accompanied by dazzling female companions, all sipping martinis or Manhattans, while mystery and adventure and confidences swirled around that paneled room like fog on a London moor.

The heroine was very, loosely modeled after a girl from Montana who was a family friend. She lived in a town with a block-long main street and a lone traffic signal. Her family were avid hunters, and I was amazed to hear this young girl's hunting stories. Tales of shooting large animals, skinning them, and packing the meat home were described in a hesitant voice as if this was too commonplace to even mention. In contrast, my family did all of its hunting and gathering in a supermarket. So when it came time to create Anna, I immediately thought of our Montana connection.

The Umbrella of Love

He was suddenly standing next to me in the rain. A man who changed my life and I never even caught his name.

I'd just arrived on a commuter flight from L.A., a journey sales-man with sample case in one hand and umbrella in the other, standing in the pouring rain waiting for the parking lot shuttle. As I checked my watch for the tenth time, I noticed him out of the corner of my eye. Tall and slim, he had his face turned up into the rain, droplets coursing down his cheeks, all the time wearing a bemused smile. He had a raincoat on, but it wasn't even buttoned. Here this guy was, standing in a near monsoon, wetter than water, and smiling up at the pelting rain. And here I stood, upset that a few drops had splashed up on my Brooks Brothers suit.

While I stared at him, he glanced over. Embarrassed that he'd caught me, I asked if he'd like to stand under my umbrella.

"Never use one," he replied.

"El Nino has been soaking us for weeks and you don't use an umbrella?"

"Never used one." He smiled, adding, "And never will."

My eyes turned back to searching for the shuttle. Still missing. What the hell I thought. I might as well bite.

"Why don't you have an umbrella?"

"It's one of those long stories."

"Well, we're not going anywhere fast," I replied with my own smile

He wiped the water off his face, a useless gesture. "Probably every good story has a woman in it somewhere, and this one's no different."

The lights of a passing car lit up his animated face. "She wasn't just any woman; she was 'the' woman for me. From the moment I saw her at work, she had full run of my imagination day and night."

"I've been there," I said.

"Small problem, though," he added. "She was engaged." He shook his head. "Lips asking to be kissed. Eyes that could light the night. A figure they model statues after."

"I'd like to meet her myself," I replied, wondering what all this had to do with umbrellas.

"But the best part of her was what was underneath. Compassionate. Intelligent. Humorous. Loving. She had this glow, this inner radiance that captured and held you like a magician on stage."

"Too bad she was engaged."

"Someone once told me, 'If you're going to fall, fall reaching'. So I reached. I talked with her, had coffee with her, worked out at the gym with her, spent every second I could with her. I wooed her like a man possessed, and yet I did it as subtly as possible, trying not to chase her off."

I saw his wistful smile in the glare of passing headlights.

"Though God knows what she saw in me, there was definitely an attraction." He shook his head and the drops flew off. "I was beginning to think that maybe I had a chance. Somehow I'd step in, rescue the damsel, and we'd ride off to a villa in Italy."

I found myself caught up in his naked emotions, his longing

tone, and I fervently hoped this wasn't going to have a bad ending... but this was real life, right?

"We spent a morning together, running in a heavy downpour, nearly oblivious to the weather, lost in flirtatious conversation." There was soft laugh. "We embraced the storm like two kids playing in rain puddles, yet all the time we sparred and danced around our growing attraction.

"She was scheduled to sing at a local church the next night where she was a member of a small band. I decided to go listen, even though I knew her fiancé would be there. I don't know, maybe I just wanted to see what kind of man she was attracted to."

He turned toward me. "There was a slight drizzle in the air, nothing like this. Feeling like a complete outsider in the small church, I took a seat in the back left side. I could see her up on the altar, the band warming up. Just before they started, I saw her look at a tall man walking up the right side of the church. It had to be the fiancé."

A car drove by and I stepped back to avoid the spray from the tires. He never moved.

"I tried to be objective. He looked like a regular guy. Dressed conservatively, smiling at the other members of the congregation. In his right hand he carried a rolled-up umbrella."

I was starting to see the connection.

"The band began to sing and they were good. But when she sang, truly the gates of heaven opened. How do you describe a voice so sweet that it should be the mandatory sound that awakens you each day and puts you to sleep each night?

"Several times during her singing, I thought she glanced over at me, but I wasn't sure. I could definitely tell when she looked at her fiancé. The smile she gave him was the kind men fight battles over. A smile that said it all." He was silent for a moment.

"As I sat there, watching her and her fiancé, I came to a crushing realization."

The parking shuttle pulled up, halting our conversation. We loaded on and I followed him to a seat in the rear. I'd spent too much time not to hear the end of this tale.

He started up immediately. "I have never been a believer in umbrellas. It goes against my whole frame of mind. Life is already too planned, too organized, and too regimented. An umbrella just seems like one more step in that direction. One more go with the crowd, have no imagination, and show no sense of adventure type of gesture.

"I watched her look at him, saw him smile back, watched his head bob with the music, and his umbrella told me we were not to be. She wanted stability, practicality, conservatism, a steady Eddie. For why else would she have fallen for a guy with an umbrella? Yet, I had offered her roller coaster romance, impromptu passion, spur of the moment excitement.

"I crept out of the church into a full downpour. Standing on the steps, I put my face up in an attempt to let the rain wash my disappointment away. It only deepened my depression."

He sat quietly for the next few moments, and then I spoke. "So you've avoided umbrellas ever since? Reminds you of lost love?"

"No, on the contrary, I did buy an umbrella about six months later."

I raised my eyebrows.

"It was just for theatrical purposes. We burned it at our wedding in Paris."

"Wedding?"

"She'd seen me leave the church. Watched me standing in the storm getting wet. And my obliviousness to the weather reminded her of our wonderful day in the rain, the whole impetuousness of our relationship from my crazy love-struck e-mails to my offers of sunsets from the bridges of Paris. She decided she wanted that spontaneity in her life and she'd never find it with someone who owned an umbrella. The next day she broke off her engagement." He laughed, rubbing the water from his hair. "So when I stand in the rain and it hammers down, it reminds me of why she loves me. It makes me feel alive, reckless, adventuresome."

I never saw that man again, but I've thought of him many times since. I still lead my humdrum existence with commuter flights four days a week, sales quotas, suits and ties - all the rat race accoutrements. But when the weather gets angry and the skies darken, I make my limited statement for reckless adventure. I no longer carry an umbrella.

* * * * *

Author's Notes: We have all seen that lone individual standing in the rain, oblivious to its effects. Haven't you ever wondered why he seemed so unaffected?

Love on the Rooftop

With the pilot's announcement that we were preparing to land, Jason Marks closed his laptop. This pause in his writing was timely since he couldn't continue until he finished the interviews. Glancing out the window from the comfort of his first class seat, he saw the lights twinkling below. He was back in the City of Lights. A city with remembrances he'd long tried to bury.

A short while later, leaning against the worn, leather seat of his taxi, Jason watched the world of Paris sail by in the dark. The passing lights were blurred by a rainy drizzle which seemed fitting since the last time he'd left Paris, the lights had also been indistinct. Only then, the lights had been obscured by his tears.

As if memories could be shaken off like drops of water, he shook his head trying to move back into the present.

The aged Mercedes' taxi rumbled over the cobblestone bridge onto the Ile St. Louis, a small island set in the middle of the Seine. The ancient buildings on either side of the street were stained black by the rain, the windows emitting elongated shafts of yellow light, reflected up from the puddles on the roadway. Few passersby were on the street at this hour and in this inclement weather.

"You can drop me here."

The grey haired cabbie half turned. "But monsieur, we are still two blocks from your rental address."

"Thanks, but I'd like to walk." He gave the driver a half-smile. "For old time's sake."

As the taxi drove off, Jason pulled the collar of his raincoat up and looked at the small bar across the street. L'Estrange. Two people came out the front door, laughing, huddled together under a bright yellow umbrella. Just two short years ago, he thought, that might have been us.

Time to let it go, he knew. Picking up his bags, he headed down rue Saint-Louis-en-L'Isle which ran the length of the island.

But forgetting wasn't that easy. The memories rose up in the form of the boulangerie where they'd bought their morning baguettes, the marché with its fresh squeezed orange juice, the fromagerie with its multiplicity of cheeses, and the petite restaurant where they'd first kissed.

By the time he neared the end of the block where he'd rented a studio flat, the old familiar ache was back. He knew he had to finish his work here quickly before the memories overpowered him.

In the distant, he spied a familiar hulking structure lit by lights at its base - the cathedral of Notre Dame. For a brief interlude, the rain stopped and the shadowy structure became more defined. The peaked roofs, central spire, and flying buttresses bespoke a different age when ignorance fostered fables and frightening tales of good and evil. This ancient specter was to be his destination tomorrow. What tales it might hold made him a bit uneasy.

As he tried to comfortably settle his six foot frame into the small bed of the rental flat, he reflected on the reason he was there. Just a week ago, he'd been doing research at the Middleton University Library Philadelphia, with Paris the farthest thought from his mind. He remembered carrying the worn, cracked leather diary over to the brown haired woman standing resolutely behind the oak counter.

"Yes, may I help you?"

"I was told that you read German. I was hoping you could help me with some translation."

"I'd be happy too." Putting on the glasses that hung from a chain around her neck, she bent over the frayed, leather bound volume. "What is this about?"

"It is a diary that recounts the travels and observations of Franz Diderhaus." Seeing that the name elicited no recognition, Jason continued. "He was a pioneer in searching out the myths of early western civilization and discrediting them."

She nodded. "I see. Well, his German scrawl is hard to decipher. Which passage are you having trouble with?"

Jason pointed to the bottom of the page. "That one. It's the last of what appears to be a list of fables that Diderhaus was going to pursue when he disappeared."

"What do you mean disappeared?"

"In 1985, at the peak of his notoriety, he simply vanished."

"How unusual." She adjusted her glasses and peered down at the book. Suddenly, she stiffened and bent even closer. When she looked up, he noticed her expression had changed, the causal air gone. She said, "You never mentioned what your interest is in this man?"

"I'm researching his life for a book I'm writing." He pointed to the page. "I'm hoping this list might give me some idea of what happened to him."

"Well, this last line translates as," her voice dropping almost to a whisper, "'do not fear the gargoyle'."

Well, that's bizarre, Jason thought. "And what is the word that follows?" he said, pointing to a collection of letters - ANArKH.

After another pause, she said, "It's not a German word. In fact, I'm not sure it's even a word." She pulled her glasses off. "I'll be right back."

In a moment, she had returned and was holding a well-thumbed, black book. She opened it to the first few pages and put on her glasses. "Yes, I thought I had seen these letters before." She looked up at Jason. "This book was written in the 1830s. In the preface here, the author describes finding these same letters engraved in stone in the dark recesses of an ancient church." She lifted the book, peering at the page. "The author writes that he 'sought to divine who could have been that soul in torment' that had inscribed these letters with 'the fatal and melancholy meaning contained in them' ".

"What meaning?"

"Apparently, before the author could pursue it further, he states, 'the wall was whitewashed or scraped down and the inscription disappeared.'" She glanced up at Jason. "It was that carving in the wall that gave him the inspiration for this book about that very same church."

"What book?"

She held it up so he could see the title. Notre Dame de Paris. "Today it's more commonly called *The Hunchback of Notre Dame.*"

Jason was shocked by the implications of where and what Diderhaus was planning on investigating. And then the second shock hit him, almost as powerful but with much less enthusiasm. To figure this out, he was going to have to go to Paris.

The librarian set the book aside, and pushed the diary toward him. "Gargoyles. Gothic messages in ancient churches. It would appear that your Mr. Diderhaus was involved in some dark happenings."

In the morning, the rain had stopped but it was still gray and cold. It held a dampness that seeped into the soul, not unlike the memories that had crept into Jason's thoughts ever since his arrival. These same reminiscences had drawn him to L'Estrange for a late breakfast. Without thinking, he had settled onto the third barstool from the left only to realize it had been where they sat. His breath caught when he saw the initials carved deep in the oak surface in front of him: JM + RM. They were as distinct as the day he had etched them. They'd laughed about having the same last initial. Jason had joked that if they ever got married, she could keep her monogrammed towels and shirts, all the while knowing she was not the type to have monogrammed anything.

A woman laughed behind him. No, it couldn't be. He swivelled around, afraid, yet hoping. But no, it was just a stranger leaning close to her companion, lost in his words. His appetite suddenly gone, Jason ordered an espresso.

The place hadn't change in the two years since he'd last been there. It had been their rendezvous, their haven. How many times had they sat on these same two stools, talking, kissing, and laughing? Life had never seemed so sweet, so alive. And never had it seemed so empty as it did now. He checked his watch. Time to go. It was a relief to walk out the door.

Jason had arranged to meet with a Father Jean, the unofficial historian of the Notre Dame church, inside the cathedral. It was awesome with its immense size, soaring ceiling, huge stained glass windows, and intricate carvings. Truly it felt like the house of God.

"I appreciate you sparing the time to see me, Father," Jason said.

"I have enjoyed your books, Mr. Marks, especially *Political Mythology* and *Myths of the Old West*," Father Jean replied, his rotund figure tightly packed into a black suit topped with a white collar. "With your special knack to search out and expose the myths and false beliefs of society, it worried me when you called. I hope you aren't here to destroy some of the ancient folklore of this wonderful cathedral?"

"Have no worries, Father. That's not why I am here. One of the major characters I'm including in my new novel vanished in 1985, and I'm trying to find out what happened to him."

Father Jean frowned. "And how is that connected to the cathedral?"

"The last entries in his diary suggest he came here." Jason paused. "He wrote something about gargoyles, and listed a series of letters - ANArKH."

With the mention of the letters, Father Jean's polite features tensed up, he placid tone sharpened. "And what makes you think he came here?"

"The gargoyle reference for one. The letters for two. The same letters that Victor Hugo found carved in the wall of this cathedral nearly two hundred years ago."

Father Jean nodded slowly. His eyes darting anywhere but to Jason's face. "Yes, I am aware that these letters, the 'Hugo phrase' we call it, were found here."

"And what does this Hugo phrase mean? And does it have any connection with the gargoyles?"

"The answer to both is I don't know." His face was more relaxed now, as if some danger had passed. He gestured to the folding chairs surrounding them in the back of the cathedral. "Why don't we sit down?"

When they were settled, Father Jean said, "What do you know of gargoyles, Mr. Marks?"

"Just what I was able to get on-line."

Father Jean nodded encouragement so Jason continued. "The word gargoyle comes from the French word 'gargouille' originally 'throat'. The English words gargle and gurgle were derived from it. The gargoyle was originally a water spout mounted on the eave of buildings, and when it rained, the water gushing from the spout would make a gargling sound. Hence, their name."

"Exactly. Their main purpose was to direct water away from the buildings so it wouldn't erode the mortar on the walls and foundations."

"Since the Middle Ages, these carved rain gutters have generated legends and folklore. What's that all about?"

Father Jean smiled knowingly. "The variety of beliefs surrounding the gargoyles are astounding. Some felt the gargoyles were actually sin frozen in stone, placed there to remind the townspeople of the evil that exists in the world."

"Do you think they are evil?"

"I lean toward the faction that viewed them as good luck creatures, frightening away evil spirits, lightening, plague, and other calamities that might threaten the cathedral and the city."

Jason pressed, "I seem to remember some legend about them being guardians that came alive at night to protect the humans entrusted to them. They had to return to their perches before the sun came up."

With a chuckle, Father Jean replied, "You've been watching too much Walt Disney. That was the gist of their cartoon show, *The Gargoyles*." He half-smiled. "Some have even theorized that uttering the Hugo phrase could bring the creatures to life." He glanced at his watch and stood up. "I'm afraid I have another appointment, Mr. Marks. Is there anything else I can do for you?"

"Thank you, but no. I'm just going to wander around and get a closer look at these stone creatures."

"If you're not afraid of spiral staircases, let me suggest the tour of the west bell tower. It puts you in close proximity to the gargoyles and gives an unparalleled view of Paris."

Father Jean started to go but then turned back, to consolidate his position. "Gargoyles are merely ornamental structures created to serve as water spouts." He smiled. "In a way, they are guardians for they have protected their buildings from time and weather. I'm sure if your Mr. Diderhaus did come here many years ago, he would have bumped up against that same reality."

As priest strode away, Jason felt a chill down his back. He knew for certain he had never mentioned Diderhaus' name to the gracious and forthright Father Jean.

"Straight out there, you can see the white turrets and cupolas of the church of the Sacré-Coeur," the guide offered in her thick French accent.

Father Jean had been truthful about one thing. The view from the bell tower was incredible even under the dark skies.

"You will notice the Seine River flowing on either side of us, for Notre Dame is built on an island, the Ile de la Cité," the guide said. "And how long has the Seine been a major fixture in Paris? Legend has it that in 1431, after Joan of Arc was burned at the stake, her ashes were thrown into the Seine. In his will, Napoleon asked to be buried on the banks of the Seine, but his request was not granted. Getting more modern, the river today supplies one-half of the drinking water for Paris."

As the tour group moved on, Jason held back to inspect the gargoyles more closely. They were fantastic. The figures could be half-animal, half-human, or completely imaginative. Frightening, exciting, life-like, grotesque, smiling, glaring, grimacing, crouching and ready to pounce upon the city. Today's horror movie monsters were tame in comparison.

The gargoyles that intrigued him the most were the winged creatures. Silent, immobile sentinels, they glared down at the city and its occupants far below. Jason had no difficulty understanding why so many myths and legends about gargoyles had sprung up.

Yet none of this was getting him closer to what had happen to Diderhaus. It was clear from Father Jean's slip that Diderhaus' inquires had lead him here, but after that he was never seen. And what of the Hugo phrase? How did that fit into any of this, if at all?

He pulled the slip of paper with the phrase printed on it from his pocket. Maybe it was a word, but in what language? He attempted various pronunciations, but they all seemed forced, none of them felt right. Behind him, he heard a rustling sound, but when he turned there were only the four gargoyles. One of them was the Spitting Gargoyle, which he'd seen many times in the travel guides. It had a human upper torso, wings on its back, and a bestial face with its tongue sticking out as if it were spitting.

He grimaced at their frozen visages. "If you guys could talk, the tales you would tell." He walked to the edge of the battlement wall and looked below on the city.

"It was right down there, two years ago, that I met Rachel Moore," he told the gargoyles. He heard a shuffling sound, but looking around he saw that he was still alone. "Have any of you gentlemen ever been in love?," he continued, "I mean really, deeply, head over heels in love?"

He glanced at the closest creature, posed to spring off the edge of the eave. It had the body of a wolf, human arms, and a canine-like face topped with horns.

"I bet you saw us. Walking hand in hand, laughing at life, stopping to kiss on every bridge we crossed." Jason was lost in his recollections. He glanced toward the gargoyles. "Wolf Man,

Spitter, or you other two, be honest. You've been looking down there for nearly eight centuries. Speak up if you have ever seen two people that were more destined to be together." His gaze moved from one to the other of the carved creatures, but the only sound came from below, the shrill whistle from a passing river boat.

It was ten minutes later, as he stepped out the tower exit, that he noticed a woman walking in his direction. There was no question about her identity. It was Rachel Moore, and if anything, she looked better than he remembered, and he remembered her as a goddess.

What is she doing here, was his first thought? Followed quickly by, I can't let her see me.

He stepped back into a shadowed recess of the wall as the woman of both his dreams and his nightmares, floated by, deeply involved in conversation with a tall, blond haired man. Her laughter still had the same pure, golden tones that had captured his heart on their first meeting.

Despite their two-year hiatus, Jason's wounds were as fresh as yesterday. Oh, Lord, he prayed, don't let her see me. As she moved off, his pounding heart began to slow down and his inner trembling subsided. That is, until the deluge of ice water dropped onto his head. He cried out more in surprise than indignation. The water had completely drenched him. Glaring up to see the source of this outrage, he saw the grinning stone face of a gargoyle, looking almost as if he had done it on purpose.

"Jason? Is that you?"

Jason had a nearly overwhelming desire to flip his middle finger at the creature that had exposed him, but instead turned to face what he had so carefully avoided for the last two years.

"It is you," Rachel said, walking toward him with a smile. God, how he loved the grace and fluidness of her movement

With as much false bravado as he could muster, Jason said, "Rachel! What a wonderful surprise." To avoid saying more, he concentrated on wiping the water off his jacket and shaking it out of his short black hair. Pointing up with his thumb, he said, "A present from above."

Rachel covered her mouth trying not to laugh. "Their spouts get obstructed, and watch out when they clear." She turned to the man who had followed her over. "Sven, this is Jason Marks... an old friend of mine."

Sven reached out to shake, but Jason held up his wet, dripping hands. "Nice to meet you, Sven."

"Don't feel bad," he said. "You are one of many the gargoyles have baptized."

"It's good to see you, Jason," Rachel said. "What brings you here?"

"I'm researching a new book. How about you?"

"Sven is helping me with a photo essay on the gargoyles of Notre Dame."

"Ya," Sven added, putting his arm around her. "Rachel has taught me much."

Jason realized he shouldn't be surprised that she had a boyfriend. At the young age of twenty-eight, Rachel was not only beautiful, but also famous for her photography. People flocked to her teaching sessions. She had the innate ability to know a good picture and how to frame it. Her photographic series titled *Faces, which* included *Faces of Iraq: the Cost of Freedom, Faces of American Poverty in the Midst of Plenty*, and *Faces of Professional Sports: Heroes and Villains*, had solidified her reputation in the photographic world.

"What a coincidence," Jason heard himself say. "My research involves the same gargoyles. Maybe we could get together and I could pick your brain." Oh, my God, he thought, did I really say that.

Rachel's expression softened for a moment and then went neutral. "I'm afraid Sven and I are already behind schedule. Maybe if we get caught up near the end of the week, I could give you a call."

"Actually, I'm almost done," Jason lied. The old ache was back so intense he could hardly focus on her words. "I'll be leaving in a day or so." Move, he told himself. Put one foot in front of the other, and move! "Well, it was good to see you, Rachel." He turned to Sven. "Nice meeting you."

With as much respectability as his soaked clothes, sloshing shoes, and trembling legs would allow, he turned and walked away from his past.

He ended up in the worst spot in Paris for him, the L'Estrange bar. And he was on the same damn stool. He gestured for another scotch, but the bartender lifted his shoulders questioningly, pointing at the five empty glasses in front of him.

Swaying on the seat, Jason again motioned for a refill. "Six is my lucky number," he slurred. And maybe with six, the ache would recede far enough to make it bearable. He felt if he stopped drinking, he'd start crying and never stop. God, she had looked good. And she had looked so happy. That's what hurt the most. The realization that she had moved on with her life, yet his life was still mired in what might have been.

Somehow it was much later and he was back on the street, but tonight it wasn't raining, it was pouring. He didn't care. He didn't really care about much of anything right then. His wandering brought him out on one of the bridges. The Seine River bubbled and swirled below him, driven by the excessive rain that had fallen for the last two weeks.

He'd long held some ridiculous idea that maybe, just maybe, Rachel would someday come back to him. Well, today had brutally ended that fantasy. He laughed at the appropriateness of it all because wasn't that what he did for a living - annihilate any myths or fantasies that people held. Well, the fantasy that had kept him going for these last two years was now completely destroyed.

He glanced around. Yes, this had been their special bridge. They'd frequently come out here and sat on the stone railing, watching the festive river boats with their strings of white lights glide past. Almost unconsciously, he found himself sitting on the railing, his feet dangling down. The river was hypnotic, almost beckoning as he stared into the angry waters below. Was it an allegory of life? Always moving, always changing, always adjusting so it could continue its course unimpeded to the distant sea. Yet here he was, unmoving, mired in yesterday, his course in life at a halt. Yes, he reluctantly decided, it's time to get back into the flow of existence.

As Jason moved to get off the railing, one hand slipped and he was suddenly falling.

What followed happened seemingly in just seconds. There was a rushing, a flapping sound, an incredible jerk on his coat, his body slamming into a hard surface, and then all went black.

The rainfall on his face awoke him. Groggily, he looked around. He was lying on the bridge walkway, flat on his back. It was a moment before he realized what must have happened. He remembered slipping but he must have fallen backwards onto the walkway instead of into the river as he'd feared.

He was still lying there when the police vehicle pulled up.

"Thank you, officers," Jason said as he climbed out of the police car in front of his studio. He'd convinced them that he'd been walking home from the bar when he'd slipped and fallen. Once they found he had no injuries and wasn't a vagrant, they'd insisted on driving him home. By this time, Jason was past inebriation and into hangover. His head felt like a drum that someone was using for a major concert.

Stepping inside his flat, he dropped his raincoat onto a kitchen chair. There was something odd about the coat. Lifting it up, he realized that the back of the coat had parallel rips high up on either side. It appeared as if the coat had snagged on something and then been torn, but he couldn't remember catching his coat on anything. Dropping his foul smelling clothes in a heap, he climbed into the shower. He was standing with a towel wrapped around his waist, toothbrush in his mouth, when he heard the knock on his door.

It had to be the police. They were back for some reason. Hesitantly, he swung the door open. There stood Rachel.

He noticed her wet hair and drenched clothes.

"Father Jean told me where to find you. I left Sven three hours ago and I've been walking in the rain ever since." She stared up at him. "We need to talk."

"Come in," he said opening the door.

She kept her distance as she entered the room.

For several extended moments they stood facing each other, neither speaking. Finally, Rachel said, "It took me a long time to get over you."

Unsure where this was leading, he said, "I'm… happy for you."

Rachel's eyes searched his face. "What are you really doing here, Jason?"

"Just what I told you, researching a book."

"You disappear for two years, and now that my life is back on track, you show up."

"I didn't really disappear. You made it obvious that you wanted me out of your life."

She sighed. "I loved you. I wanted to spend the rest of my life with you. But my work, my pictures are so stressful, so depressing, that I need a refuge. A place where I can retreat and be comforted by someone who can make me believe that there is still some magic left in this out of control world." She gently shook her head. "I wanted someone who thought that angels could be laughing, and that unexplainable wonderful things could and would happen. And never question the why, but just enjoy that they did."

After a pause, Jason said softly, "I thought the magic in our relationship was enough."

"So did I, but I was afraid that in time your outlook on life – your 'if I can't prove it's real, then it doesn't exist' attitude – would wear me down."

"But that's my job and… it's what I believe in," he said slowly. "I wish it weren't."

They stared at each other for a long moment. Gradually, her frown receded and her eyes softened.

"Seeing you… seeing you in this town," her voice faltered. "It's too much." She dropped her head. "There hasn't been a day that I haven't thought about you, wondered about you, cried about you."

He saw her shoulders start to shake; she was crying. Stepping toward her, he put his arms around her and pulled her tight. It felt so natural and she fit so perfectly. Smelling her hair and feeling the warmth of her body blending with his, the old memories flooded in. Now she wasn't the only one crying.

How long they stood like that he wasn't sure, but finally he felt her shaking stop. He loosened his hold on her and leaned back to see her face.

"Rachel, I…"

Before he could finish, they were kissing. At first he held back, unsure of what he should do. But what started soft and slow, soon evolved into uncontrollable passion, as if in this one moment they had to make up for the last two years. Jason kissed her with an intensity he'd never known; running his hands over the curves and valleys he never thought he'd touch again. Over and over, she murmured his name as she melted her body into his, matching his fervor and ferocity. The emotional ups and downs of the night were gone. Nothing mattered but right now. Their mouths still locked, he lifted her and carried her to the bedroom.

The sound of laughter woke him the next morning. It was a group of school kids passing by his window.

Lying on his back, he couldn't help smiling. There was an inner peace, a feeling of completeness he'd not felt for years. Turning, he noticed that the bed was empty.

He called out, "Rachel?" but there was no response. On the bedside table he saw a note.

Dear Jason,

Last night was wonderful, but today is reality. I have to protect myself, surround myself with people who seek the wonders of life, not try and disprove them. Your staunch belief system is not good for me. In the end, I wouldn't be able to survive.

If we happen to meet, let it be as friends and nothing more, as much as I wish it were.

As for your research regarding the gargoyles, there is a volunteer caretaker named Joseph. We have become really close and there is nothing about the gargoyles that he doesn't know. He has a wonderful outlook on life, and is a true believer of all the mystery and enchantment around us. Maybe some of it will rub off on you.

> *Always yours, Rachel*

Several hours and a shattered dream later, Jason was back at the cathedral for a noon appointment with the volunteer caretaker.

"Hello, Mr. Marks. I'm Joseph. You wanted to talk with me?"

Joseph had one of those ageless European faces, with flat planes, minimal wrinkles, and thick silver hair. He stretched out a hand and smiled. Jason noted that the smile didn't extend into his eyes.

After they shook, Joseph said, "How can I help you, Mr. Marks."

"Please call me, Jason. I am trying to find out what happened to a man named Hans Diderhaus. My sources lead me to believe he came here, apparently to study the gargoyles and try to solve the mystery of the Hugo phrase."

Joseph's smile vanished. "Yah, I knew Hans. What is your interest in him?"

"I am writing an exposé of various American and European myths that have crept into our society. Since Mr. Diderhaus was one of the foremost leaders in this field, I'd hoped to include the details of his life."

Joseph nodded. "Yah, he was that. And from what I have read about you, it would appear that you are following in his footsteps." He paused looking down at his scuffed work boots. "Come, Jason. We can talk of Hans later. Let me show you my wards, my stone family. Since Notre Dame has more than five thousand gargoyles, we will only visit my favorites."

They spent the afternoon climbing stairs, trudging along hidden passages, crawling thorough spaces too small to stand. He learned that the carvings that served as water spouts were gargoyles, while those that were merely ornamental were called grotesques. And amongst the five thousand, no two were alike. Once again Jason was overwhelmed with the creativity of the artisans that shaped this world of stone beings.

After an especially difficult climb onto a rooftop, Joseph pointed to a very small carving. "That is Dedo, the cross-toed gargoyle. Tired of all these evil-looking gargoyles, legend has it that a nun named Marie Therese snuck in dressed as a man. She carved this cute little guy and hid him up here where only God could see him." He paused. "He wasn't discovered until centuries later when a small boy, lost in the cathedral, rolled down this roof and was saved from falling by grabbing Dedo."

Joseph led Jason back into the cathedral. "That Dedo is a nice story, yes? Well, Hans was going to try and disprove that legend, along with many others related to these creatures."

"Is that why he came here?"

"Yah. He wanted to dispel all the theories, stories, and legends regarding the gargoyles." Joseph gave a harsh laugh. "He was a fool, meddling in things he knew nothing about. Leaving a path of disenchantment and dashed dreams wherever he went."

"Why are you so bitter?" Jason asked coldly. "These stone creations are just ornamental water spouts, nothing more."

Joseph slowly shook his head. "You are so much like him. I pity you." He paused, and then put his hand on Jason's shoulder. "Let an old man give you a piece of advice, Jason. Don't continue his work. It will only lead to pain and loss as it did for Hans."

"You know what happened to him?"

"Yes. Shortly after his visit here, he drowned in the Seine."

"What?!"

"It never made the papers. Bad for tourism."

Jason hung his head. The day had started poorly, and now it was getting worse.

Glancing up, he said, "Did he ever speak to you about the Hugo phrase?"

"I heard him yell it once. Just before he died," Joseph said.

"He spoke the word? And you were there?"

"Hans is dead and gone. Let's leave it at that," Joseph said firmly.

Jason thought of the myriad of questions he still wanted to ask, but it was clear that the discussion regarding Diderhaus was over.

"How do you know Rachel?" Jason said, hoping to keep the old man talking.

Joseph smiled, and this time that feeling reached up into his eyes. "Rachel Moore and I have worked very closely for the last three weeks while she has been photographing my stone children."

"What did she think of the gargoyles?"

"She was entranced by them," he said, "and, to no surprise, they grew to love her. She is an amazing young woman."

"You are preaching to the preacher, Joseph."

"Yes, she talked about you."

"Something good, I hope."

Joseph inspected Jason's face closely, finally saying, "More melancholy than good." He remained silent for a long moment then appeared to come to a decision. "Jason, I am going to show you where Hans Diderhaus died. It will explain many things. We will go there tonight, after I finish my chores."

It was nearly nine when Joseph was finally free, and another hour before they were at the site of Hans Diderhaus' death. They stood under one of the arched bridges that spanned the Seine. A slight drizzle had settled in and the temperature had dropped. A stone pathway or quay ran along both sides of the

Seine. The side of the quay on the river edge was also stone and sloped steeply down into the river ten feet below.

Joseph moved to the edge and stared down into the sickly brownish-green water.

"It was at this spot that Hans died," he said.

Jason glanced around. They stood in the shadow of the bridge, out of the rain, but surrounded by a dank, musty smell.

"He fell in?"

"Not exactly. It was more of an experiment. He wanted to test his beliefs. He was beginning to think that his whole life had been a lie." Joseph stepped back from the edge. "And that night Hans Diderhaus died."

"What was this experiment?" Jason asked as he moved to the edge. He was still staring into the river when something struck the back of his head and everything went black.

The first thing Jason felt when he came to was a tight pressure around his chest and a cold damp sensation against his face. Opening his eyes, he realized the pressure was a rope and he was dangling just above the river, his face against the stone wall. Looking up, he saw that Joseph was holding the end of the rope.

"Joseph, what the hell are you doing? Pull me up! For God's sake, pull me up! I can't swim."

"You asked about Hans Diderhaus' experiment. Well, this was it. He tied a rope to one of these posts along the river, lowered himself over the side, and then made a choice. Did he let go and find the truth or did he climb back up and never know?"

"Are you crazy? Pull me up. If I have a choice, pull me up!"

"Do you know why I brought you here tonight? Why I am giving you this opportunity?"

Jason grabbed the rope and tried to haul himself up, but it was covered with moss. The wall of the quay was too steep to climb. Buy some time, he reasoned. Someone is bound to see us.

"I am giving you this chance for several reasons. The first is that Rachel Moore still cares very deeply for you. She may not admit it, but in our conversations I could tell. I would love to see her happy."

Jason felt the rope slip down slightly and now his feet were in the water. "Joseph I love her too. Pull me up. Please, pull me up!"

"The other reason is that your life is false, Jason. It is destroying things which should never be touched. There are truths that may seem impossible to you, even unimaginable, yet they are real. And if I can convince you, maybe you will leave them alone."

Keep him talking, someone has to come by, Jason thought, so he said, "Truths like what?"

"The gargoyles for one. They come alive at night and soar in the skies. Amongst their duties is watching over the river. Diderhaus discovered this, and it shattered his inflexible belief system. But at the same time, it filled him with an appreciation and a fascination for these miracles of life."

When there was no reply, Joseph said, "Do you believe me, Jason?"

"Yeah, Joseph. I believe you. Pull me up and let's go watch them fly."

"Jason, Jason. You are not listening, but no matter, I will give you two choices. I pull you back up and you never know if there is more than what you believe. Or I let the rope go, and you see if there are mysteries beyond your wildest imagination."

"I chose number one. Pull me up."

"If that's your final choice, I will pull you up. But before I do, ask yourself what have you got to lose if I let you go. Your life?" He paused. "Do you really enjoy having your life's goal the destruction of all that is enchanting? And what about Rachel. Is your life worth living without her?"

"Good questions, Joseph. Pull me up, and let's talk about them."

"You're missing the point, Jason. The real question is what might you gain if I let you go." He waited a moment, and then said, "Rachel Moore. She wants you, but not as you are. She wants a man that truly believes in more than unbending reality."

Jason hung from the rope. It was true, and as the person he was now, he would never be that man. And what if Joseph were right? What if everything he held as truth was false? That wonders he'd never imagined existed? Knowing that would change him, and give him a chance of getting her back. One small problem.

"How the hell can I get Rachel back if I'm on the bottom of the Seine?" he yelled.

"You almost ended up there last night," Joseph said.

"How did you know about that?"

"A stone creature with talons told me." The rope dropped a bit more. "Make your choice quickly, Jason, since I'm having trouble holding you."

Oh, my God, Jason thought. There is no reasoning with him. And then it hit him. Joseph had done this before. He had been at this same location when Didherhaus drowned or how else would he have known what happened? How else would he have heard Diderhaus call out the Hugo phrase? Unless...

"Joseph, what year were you born?" Jason asked.

He heard the shout above him. "That's the spirit, lad. I was born in 1933."

"And how do you pronounce the Hugo phrase?"

"You pronounce the phrase as it appears, except the 'H' is silent, "Joseph replied.

"Hans didn't exactly die, did he Joseph? It was more like he was reborn?" Jason glanced down once more at the surging water below him. "I've made my choice. Let me go."

As Joseph released the rope, Jason yelled, "ANArKH!" and then he was enveloped in a maelstrom of water.

Rachel checked her watch once more. It wasn't like Joseph to be late for an appointment, especially when he stressed how important it was. And why had he picked L'Estrange as the meeting place? Of course, he knew about her history here with Jason from their discussions. As she lifted her glass of wine, she stared once more at the initials scratched into the bar. Tracing the letters with her finger, a wistful smile appeared. After the other night with Jason, she'd told Sven that she needed time apart. Actually, she needed time to recover from her encounter with Jason. How could she still feel so strongly about him after two years?

Suddenly, the heavy wooden front door was flung open sending a cold breeze flooding through the cozy room. Turning, she saw Jason standing in the doorway. Soaked to the skin, his raincoat a shredded mess, she watched as his eyes anxiously swept the room and then found her. She saw him smile and his eyes fill with joy. In two bounds he was across the room and pulling her from the stool in a crushing embrace.

"I'm a believer," he said as he hugged her. "Miracles, magic, gargoyles - they all exist."

She stepped back, examining his face. Something was different, some indefinable change. She could see it in his eyes and in his smile. The haunted look she'd seen just the other day had vanished. "What's happened to you? And where is Joseph?"

Jason wiped the water off his face, and shook it out of his hair. "His name isn't Joseph. It's Hans Diderhaus." Glancing down at his clothes, he smiled, "And as for my clothes, Spitter got a little over exuberant…" He stopped, realizing what he'd been about to say. She would never believe him, even with all her broad-mindedness. He couldn't believe it himself and he had lived it. Better to tone down the truth.

"Are you okay?" she asked.

He nodded. "Tonight my beliefs were opened to a new reality." Pulling her close, he continued, "And thank God, it's not too late to enjoy it."

She leaned back, staring up at him. "Who are you?" she said with a half-smile.

"I'm the man that has given up everything I believed in to become the person you want."

It was a moment and then with a widening smile, she said, "Well, I guess this is a night for miracles and magic, because miraculously, I know that I still love you. And magically, the biggest thing that was keeping us apart seems to have disappeared."

As he enveloped her in his arms, he heard a distant flapping sound. In the old days, he would have attributed it to a banging shutter. Now, with his new found viewpoint, he wondered if it might be another stone carved creature streaking across the night sky.

*   *   *   *   *

Author's Note: My wife and I spent a wonderful ten days in Paris in the late 1990s, living in a small apartment on the Ile St. Louis, just as described in the story, and it truly is a city of love.

Notre Dame was one island over from our apartment and we spent a long day there. The gargoyles were captivating and it got me interested in their history. Other than coming alive and flying, my description of their past and their appearances is true. Little Dedo does exist as do all the rest of them. And gargoyles periodically do dump water on passing sightseers.

The inscription of "ANArKH" was actually found by Victor Hugo on a wall in Notre Dame while he was writing "The Hunchback of Notre Dame." So intriguing was this phrase that it begged to be used in some context in this story.

Secondhand Memories

My life started five days ago. I have been told that I was in a motor vehicle accident and that I am lucky to be alive. But how lucky can I be when I have lost my entire past. I have been informed that it's the head trauma that created this amnesia, and with luck - which is probably all used up by now - my memory should return. Well, the cracked ribs, the broken leg, the fractured sternum are all mending, but so far my memory remains a blank except for the last five days. The memory problem would be concerning enough, but in these last five days I have discovered that I have a wife I do not remember, and I have fallen in love with a nurse who is married. So I have more than just memory concerns.

"Good morning."

I shifted my view from the tube in my chest to the figure in the doorway. It was her, my nurse.

"Karen. Good morning."

"How are you feeling today?"

"Like a million dollars... green and wrinkled."

"What?" she asked with a tilt of her head.

"Forget it. Bad joke."

She smiled. "Humor is a good sign." She put a blood pressure cuff on my arm and inflated it. "Physical therapy will be by after breakfast, so let's get you ready."

For just a moment, I stared up at her and thought how easy it would be to wake up each morning looking into those brown eyes with their flecks of gold. Then I quickly looked away before I blurted out something really embarrassing. I had to be realistic. I was married. And how would I know that fact since I have no memory? Well, let's move back five days ago when my brain finally came back on line and I discovered that all its files had been deleted.

"Excuse me... nurse," I said. "I'm sorry but I can't seem to remember your name."

She was tall with long brown hair and looks that should be unforgettable. "It's Karen, and don't feel embarrassed. With your head injury, your memory is going to be a bit shaky."

"What memory? I have no recollection of anything." I tried to be calm and clinical. "What did the doctor say about my memory returning?"

"Dr. Lewis wasn't sure. He mentioned a number of possibilities, including it might all come back very soon."

"What were the other 'possibilities'?"

She reached behind me and readjusted my pillow. A faint smell of gardenias enveloped me. "It might only partially return... or it might never come back."

As objectively as possible, I wondered what it would be like to re-start my life with no prior memories. No past recollections of family or friends. No work abilities. Good times, bad times, moments with loved ones - all gone. This would be incredibly traumatic if everything was permanently stripped from my memory. Even a fire that gutted your house and incinerated all its contents still left you with a history.

The nurse must have read my mind. "Steve, you have to be positive. You're alive, you're going to heal, and most, if not all, of your memory should come back." She paused. "It's just going to take time."

"But what if nothing comes back?"

"Some people would love to have the chance for a 'do over'. Rebuild their lives. Rearrange their priorities."

She was moving toward the door when my words stopped her. "Before you go, can you tell what you know about my life? Anything would be helpful."

Karen perched on the edge of the bedside chair. "Do you remember us talking about your life before?

"No," I said, feeling stupid.

"Well, don't feel awkward. I am here to help you recover, and a large part of that recovery is getting your memory back."

I nodded.

"I don't know a lot but here is what I have gathered. You are forty-one and married."

I jerked upright. "I'm married?" Seeing her bland expression, I added, "You told me this before, didn't you?"

"I did, but we can discuss it as many times as you need." Karen gave me a gentle smile. "If it helps, she seems to be a very nice person."

"She's been here?"

"She was a regular bedside fixture after the accident."

"Then where is she now?"

The nurse paused. "She had to fly to Europe. Apparently her mother was on a trip and became seriously ill. With you on the mend, she knew you would understand."

I lay back in the bed.

"I'll check in on you later."

I lifted my hand in a distracted farewell, lost in my mental fear games. What would it be like to live with a woman I knew nothing about, had no feelings for, and who was in fact a total stranger? Even scarier, I wondered if a head injury could somehow alter whom I might chose for a wife.

Somewhere in all of this, I fell back to sleep. When I awoke, Karen was back checking how much drainage there was from my chest tube.

She saw me looking at her. "How are you doing?"

"Physically, I'm mending. Mentally, I'm scared to death." My eyes flew around the room and then settled back on her. "There's nothing in my brain except a void that I am gradually filling with despair."

"Is there some way I can help?"

Where the idea came from I still don't know, but it was suddenly the most natural request. 'Yes, there is. I need some memories to fill this emptiness. Something to think about besides my problems."

"Sounds reasonable. Where are you going to get these memories?"

I gave her my most winning smile. "Hopefully, from you." Before she could respond, I rushed on. "Tell me about yourself, your life, your past. And let's see if I can remember any of it tomorrow."

She slowly shook her head. "I've had some strange requests, but nothing like this."

"I realize this is reaching, but I truly think if I could listen to someone else's past, share their memories…"

I could see it in her eyes. She just needed a little push. "I noticed your wedding ring," I said, "where did you and your husband meet?"

She put her hands up in surrender. "Okay, you win." She settled into the chair, and I saw a half-smile play across her lips. "I met my husband at the hospital. He was doing research here."

"Do you remember your first date?"

"Vividly. We went to lunch together at a small romantic restaurant. I had French onion soup, he had Caesar salad, and neither of us ate a thing." She laughed. "He later told me that his friends had a rating system for how a date had gone. The highest rating was 'knee to knee, forehead to forehead'."

"Is that some kind of sexual position?" I bantered.

She laughed again. "Hardly. It refers to those couples that are so caught up in the moment, so attracted to each other, that when they sit at a table, they are…"

"Knee to knee, forehead to forehead," I said, finishing it for her.

"Yes. And that was what our first date was like.

Karen and I talked for another fifteen minutes. I learned about her high school, her stint as a song leader, the young men in her life, her infatuation with the nursing profession, and then she had to leave.

"Can you come back, maybe during a break?"

She stood up. "Sure, if you think it's helping."

"Well, let's see if I can retain any of this.

Near the end of her shift, Karen reappeared. "I have some time before I have to leave, and thought you might want to talk some more."

I arranged myself into a sitting position. "You mentioned that first date with your husband." I paused. "See my short term memory is on the mend." I gave her a quick smile. "Anyway, after that initial date, was it a smooth road to marriage?"

"Not quite. We had a few obstacles. I had just recently separated and he was living with someone."

"You were married before?"

"At eighteen. It was a means of escape from home." She sighed. "A nice guy but it just didn't work."

"How long did you date your present husband before he proposed?"

Her smile had just a touch of melancholy. "He asked me to marry him five years after we got married."

"Run that by me again."

She glanced at her watch. "We had been going out for about two years. There was an argument over something I can't even remember. The real cause was that our relationship had reached the point where it either went to the next level or it died out." She stared off at some point over my head. "We were both very much in love, but afraid to take that next step. The fight just brought it to a head. In the end, we decided to break up."

"That was a mutual decision?"

"Oh, it was and it wasn't. It hurt tremendously but if he wasn't going to commit then I needed to move on. Once I left, he started to have second thoughts. Like maybe I really was the one for him. But then he worried that he might only want me because he couldn't have me. He decided he would stay away for three months. If at the end of that time, he still felt this strongly, then he would find me and ask me to marry him."

"Sounds logical, and yet not," I said.

"He wanted to make sure that I knew what his plans were so he came over to talk. During the drive to my apartment, he began to worry I wouldn't want to get married under any circumstances, especially since I'd recently gotten divorced."

"Understandable," I said.

"So after a bit of small talk, he decided to test the waters." She looked straight at me. "He asked me what I thought about getting married."

"Oh, no."

"Oh, yes. I immediately threw my arms around his neck and said I would love to. It was a moment or two before he realized what had happened, and another few moments before he decided that if he didn't know now, he never would. And so we were engaged." She glanced at her wedding ring. "Of course, he didn't tell me about this misunderstanding until after we were married. Five years and two kids later, at a large family gathering, in front of more than twenty surprised relatives, he got down on one knee and asked me if I would be his wife."

She stood up and smiled. "I told him no, of course." And then she left.

I loved her stories. Not only for the content, but to hear her laugh, watch her frown, or see her get excited. That was the real beauty of these recollections. Over the next couple of days, she filled in more of her life and more of her marriage. She spoke about their honeymoon in the Virgin Islands, just the two of them sailing from island to island. White beaches, palm trees, crystal clear water, and romantic restaurants in small bays.

"We loved the evenings, lying out on the deck, sipping wine, staring at a million stars," she said. "The one downside was that the nights were so hot we had to leave all the hatches open. The mosquitoes ate us alive that first night, so we bought mosquito repellent. It smelled like gasoline but it was the only way to survive. We would rub it all over our bodies before going to bed. Not the best aphrodisiac. I think it left me with a permanent mental scar." She paused. "I get a romantic feeling whenever I'm filling my car with gas."

I laughed till my broken ribs ached.

She and her husband loved to travel so I heard about their numerous trips to Tahoe, Hawaii, New York, the Florida Keys, and Paris. Early on, they especially loved to camp on the deserted beaches of Baja, along the Sea of Cortez. Long, languid days in the sun with just a tent, two dogs, and a cooler full of beer.

My past memory remained AWOL, but the short term memory was working well and everything she confided to me seemed to stay. As I learned more and more about her life, my sense of loss, of having no past, seemed to weigh less and less on me. Her stories were giving me a focus or a base that in some strange way was filling my void. And these talks gave me a format for what questions I should ask my own wife, and what memories I should ask her to fill in.

During all this, my wife called several times but it was always bad timing. Either I was out in the halls with physical therapy or off getting some tests done. I tried calling her cell phone but apparently she had no coverage in the area where her mother was recovering.

I was four days into this new life of shared memories when Cheryl, another of one of my nurses, peeked into the room. "You have a visitor."

I pushed myself higher up in the bed. "Send them in."

A short, thin man with salt and pepper hair, and turtle shell glasses walked in. "Hello, Steve. The nurse said you might not remember me."

My vacant stare said it all to him.

"Well, then I guess we do have to start over." He stuck out his hand. "I'm Charles Whitmore, your literary agent and, I like to think, your best friend."

"Please to re-meet you, Charles," I said shaking his hand. "I'm a writer?" I paused. "I'm sure someone mentioned that, but until recently my memory hasn't been retaining anything." I pointed to the bedside chair. "Please, grab a seat, and tell me about myself."

He settled into the chair. "First, call me Charley. And second, I am so glad to see that you are doing well. There was a time when we weren't sure you were going to make it."

"Fortunately, I can't remember any of that. In fact, there is very little I remember. So anything you can tell me about me would be great."

Charlie appeared perplexed and after a moment said, "There is so much, I'm not really sure where to start."

I needed to prime the pump. "You mentioned I was a writer."

"Yes and a very good one. Three books on the *New York Times* bestseller list. Hollywood filmed one of your books and has taken an option on another."

"What do I write about?"

"Fictional slices of life. Love stories involving unlikely couples facing overwhelming odds. Real gut-wrenching stuff." He hesitated, looking a bit sheepish. "They're not really my kind of read, but the public loves them."

I was starting to like Charley. "How long have we known each other?"

"Nine years, give or take. There's not much we haven't shared during that time."

"So you know my wife?"

His smile was wide and genuine. "Yes, I do and very well."

For some reason, I felt a stab of regret. "They tell me she was here while I was in the ICU, but I can't remember."

"I don't have to tell you or maybe I do," he said as his eyes lit up. "You are married to a special woman. Adjectives like looks, intelligence, or personality are totally inadequate. You could take her home to mom, to a church social, or go clubbing in Vegas, and she'd fit in everywhere, and be loved by everyone." He paused. "They say God watches over fools. Well, He was sure watching out for you when He sent her your way."

I dreaded the answer to my next question. "Do we have any children?"

"No, but there was some talk awhile back."

"What happened?"

Charley eyes roamed around the room finally stopping at a point above my heard. "You've had a real shock to you system, Steve. It might be better if we wait..."

I cut him off. "I'd like to hear it now."

Charley took off his coat and laid it over the back of his chair. "Okay then. Well, the truth is that your life had taken a new direction. Hollywood was courting you. The TV talk shows wanted interviews. The publishers had you on the road all the time, and when it wasn't book signing time, it was let's enjoy my fame time. Instead of staying home and writing, you were constantly traveling, going to parties, and mingling with the Hollywood set. Initially your wife was right there, but slowly she burned out." He leaned forward. "She saw you being pulled toward Hollywood and away from a home and family with her. She finally told you to make a choice."

This didn't sound good.

"You argued that you had spent years of your life slaving over your word processor, and now it was time to enjoy the benefits. She agreed, only she saw the benefits as having more free time to start a family."

Sadness rose up in me. "What did I do?"

"You made a bad decision." He stared at me for a moment. "If it's any consolation, I think the real problem was that success and Hollywood blurred your perception of what was important and not important. It distorted all of your decisions. It changed who you were." He paused again. "The two of you tried to work it out but Hollywood had its hold on you, and no amount of marriage counseling made a difference. You separated shortly afterwards."

"When did this happen?"

"Four months ago. She asked you to move out and you went to Los Angeles." He shrugged his shoulders.

I glanced out the window at the tree lined hill. "What am I doing back in Carmel?"

"You came to your senses and flew up here to talk with her."

"And?"

"And it didn't go well. Voices were raised, egos were bruised, and she walked out in the middle of your reconciliation dinner. I think the word 'divorce' was used near the end."

"Oh, man," I said shaking my head.

"On the way back to your hotel, you were hit by a drunk driver." He spread his arms out. "And you ended up here."

"No wonder my wife rushed back to see her mother. I'm surprised she even bothered to visit me."

Dr. Lewis entered the room. "Good evening, Steve."

After I introduced Charley, Lewis said, "Can you excuse us for a few minutes, Mr. Whitmore, while I examine Steve?"

"Hey, I have to get going anyway. Steve, I'll see you in the morning." As he stood up, he pulled a book from his brief case. "Thought you might want some reading material. Try this. It's your latest novel."

Dr. Lewis finished his evaluation and had been gone about

twenty minutes when Karen arrived.

"Hi. Thought I'd check in and see how you are doing."

"Not so good. I just learned I can be a real jerk."

She stared at me for a few moments, and then softly said, "Do you want to talk about it?"

"And tell you how I let a wonderful woman get away because I had become an egotistical, selfish, asshole?" I shook my head. "I wanted so much to get my memory back. Now I'm not so sure."

"That's the wrong attitude. Whatever you were or have done, there is always time to make a change."

I shrugged my shoulders. "I hope you're right." Gesturing toward the door, I said, "How come I have no visitors? Charley, who just left, has been my only one."

Karen explained that Dr. Lewis felt patients with severe amnesia recovered faster if they weren't stressed by friends who kept asking them if they remembered this or that. When they couldn't remember, it often seemed to depress the patient rather than help. He let Charley visit but turned the others away.

"Not sure I agree with that. Sitting here alone all day is depressing." I paused, "I will say, though, that talking with you, has been a great help." I ran my hand through my hair. "I can't explain it, but since speaking with you I don't have as much anxiety about the future, if that makes any sense."

She smiled. "Yes, it does. As a nurse, we try to heal not only the body but also the mind."

We were both silent for a while, as I tried to put my conversation with Charley behind me. After a deep breath in and out, I moved to a new topic. "Do you have any children?"

It was a moment before she replied, "No, but we are working on it."

"Nice work if you can get it," I said with a smile.

She put her head back and laughed. The line of her neck, the smoothness of her skin, the prominence of her jaw line, and the melody of her voice all brought a sudden realization. I liked this woman, and not just as a nurse. She fascinated me; she bought life and excitement to my days. And she made me realize that I had not forgotten what is beautiful and desirable in life. I made a promise to ask Whitmore if he knew what had made me fall in love with my wife.

She saw my serious expression. "What's wrong?"

"Just thinking what it's going to be like when I meet my wife."

"A little scary?"

"More than a little. I have no memory of her at all. No memory of our times together. And the questions I have are endless: Will I still be attracted to her? Will she have any feelings for me? And where do we go from here?" I paused. "Yeah, I am a little scared."

"If there is any love left in your relationship, I'm sure you can work things out."

The following afternoon, both Charlie and Karen stepped in together. As I set my book down, Charlie pointed at it. "So what do you think of the book?"

I shrugged. "The story is actually pretty good, but it's not worth losing a wife over. Nothing I could ever write would be worth that."

"Now that sounds like the man I knew pre-Hollywood," Charlie replied. "There is hope for you yet."

Karen picked up the book and paged through it. "Looks interesting. I'll have to read it sometime."

"I'll leave it for you, and even sign it," I said. "That and $4.00 will get you a cup of coffee at Starbucks."

Two days later, it was time for me to be discharged. I was told that I had gotten maximum hospital benefit and the rest of my therapy would be done as an outpatient. For the tenth time I tried to reach my wife, but her cell phone just sent me to her message box. I called Charley, who had come by every day, and told him about my pending discharge. He took this news like a true friend.

"Steve, finish your recovery here in Carmel. We have a small guest house you can use. Besides, there's nothing for you back in LA? I'll pick you up in two hours."

The offer was great, but the reason behind it was incredibly depressing. I was forty-one and all that I had waiting for me was four sheet-rock walls in an impersonal apartment complex. Oh, yeah, there were some social climbing women, a few loser parties, and the ever present Hollywood groupies surviving off of other peoples' success. Yes, staying up here did sound like the right move. And maybe I could get to know this wife that Charley raved about. Although I knew little if anything about myself, I couldn't accept the real me as such a buffoon to fall for the glitter of tinsel town. A mid-life crisis or some such thing made more sense. Hopefully, along with my memory loss, whatever anxieties had precipitated my emotional crash had also been lost.

I was shaved, showered, and sitting in a wheelchair when Charley arrived.

"You look great, Steve." He grabbed the handles and turned me toward the doorway. "Time to join the real world. But before you do, your nurse, Karen wanted to wish you well."

And I had a few things I needed to say to her.

Karen walked in wearing her starched white uniform, and said hi to both of us. "Looks like I caught you just in time. I wanted to say goodbye."

"I was hoping you would stop by." I turned to Charlie. "I know

I mentioned this before but I can't say it enough. This woman is the reason I have survived this whole nightmare."

"Well, if I ever get stuck in here, I will be asking for Karen," Charlie said, flashing a grin at her.

"Ah, Charlie," I said pointedly, "Could you give us a moment?" I subtly nodded toward the door.

He gave me a knowing look and then stepped out of the room.

"Karen, I want to thank you for everything." I paused. I wanted to tell her how much I had needed her stories, her presence, and her personality these past five days. And now that I was leaving the hospital, I didn't want that to end. I wasn't ready for what she said next.

"I'm the one that needs to thank you, Steve. Although I never spoke of it, my husband and I have had serious problems lately and I thought things were over. Spending these days with you has helped me remember why I fell in love with him. I am going to take time off and we are going to try and rekindle our relationship." She put her hand on my arm. "Now what were you going to say?"

What could I say? She was on her way back to love, and I had no right to upset that. She deserved better from me. Yet I couldn't let her leave without saying something. "At another time and another place, I wouldn't let you go."

She squeezed my arm and started to speak.

"Okay, you two," Charley boomed stepping into the room. "Time to pull nurse and patient apart, and reunite patient with wife." He handed me his cell phone. "Your wife is back in town and said to call her when you were leaving. She'll meet us at the hospital entrance."

"Excuse me for a moment," I said, turning the wheelchair away. I knew the number by heart now and quickly dialed it, feeling as nervous as a kid asking his first date out. It started ringing and this time was quickly picked up.

"Hello, Steve." I froze. The voice seemed so familiar and then I knew. Spinning around, I saw Karen holding her cell phone to her ear. She smiled tentatively as she closed the phone. "I think it's that other time and place you mentioned." Her smile widened, spreading into her eyes.

Charley held both hands up to forestall any response I had. "If you're upset, blame me. It was my idea." He glanced over at Karen. "When I heard that your memory was gone, I thought if I could put you two together, give you a chance to rediscover each other, maybe, just maybe the magic might return." He gestured toward Karen. "She was originally against it. But as you two shared more and more, she decided to let it play out."

It took several moments for all this to sink in, and then I realized what a gift I had been given. With tears in my eyes, I pulled Karen to me and hugged her like there was no tomorrow, only today. And in this today, there was no room for Hollywood or midlife crisis. There was just this woman that I adored. "I am so sorry," I whispered. "Please forgive me."

I had lost my memory, but thank God I had found my heart.

* * * * *

Author's Note: The memories that Karen shared with Steve were actually a retelling of my courtship with my wife, all the way down to the bungled engagement. One of my old professors use to say, "To be specific is to be terrific." Well, I wasn't very specific in the conversation which lead to my engagement, but the results have been terrific.

In the Blink of an Eye

In the blink of an eye, life can all go awry. – Unknown

Sam Lakota stepped down from the train and dropped his bags onto the scuffed, wooden platform. In front of him stood a squat, single story building, clothed in faded red paint. Above the entrance hung a once black sign with white letters, "Welcome to River Bottom, Kansas".

"Yeah, I really have hit bottom," he murmured to himself. Pulling his damp shirt away from his back, he then wiped the sweat from his forehead

He wasn't sure what was worse: the incredible heat or the humidity. God, how do people live in this climate, he wondered? A noise caused him to turn. Descending the steps was an eye-catching young woman. He lifted a hand to help his fiancée, Mary, climb down.

"Thank you," she said, landing lightly on the platform. Slowly, she spun around, like a ballerina on a stage.

"It's so good to be home!" she said, entwining her arm into his. "I know you're going to love it here. Just give it time".

Sam just nodded. A lifetime wouldn't be enough time, he decided.

"I'm going to use the lady's room before I call my parents to pick us up," she said as she kissed him on the cheek. "Can I borrow your cell phone? My battery's dead."

He pulled out his phone and noticed his battery was low. "Here, there's probably just enough left to call them."

"If not, I'm sure there's a pay phone in the building," she said, heading for the station.

What had he got himself into? He glanced around, trying to see the place through Mary's eyes. What he saw was a small, down-trodden town with one story buildings interspersed amongst an occasional two story structure, all fronting onto a two-block long main street. Behind the buildings and the scattered homes, he could see miles of open, windblown prairie with tumble-weeds the seeming crop of choice.

Again he wondered what the hell he was doing here, but he knew the answer. Mary! Even though he had offered to fly her parents out to California, she'd been adamant that they come to Kansas and see where she had grown up.

Sagging buildings with blistered paint, cracked and parched earth, stark bare trees - all encased in dust. People didn't come here to grow up. They came here to dry up and blow away.

He had an ocean view condo, sun drenched beaches, gourmet restaurants, professional sports teams, a batch of close friends, and a thriving job. Now he was expected to give it all up and move to this dust haven?

He looked around once more at the bleak, desolate, landscape. Despite the wide open spaces, he felt like he was in a cage whose door was gradually closing. In contrast to this limitless waste land, in his mind's eye he saw the blue water, the green fertile fields, the sparkling beaches, and the tree-shrouded mountains of California.

To make it worse, he was still uncomfortable about this whole marriage thing. Since graduating from high school, he'd never had a girlfriend longer than a few months. Talk about a rolling stone, he was a rock on steroids charging down the dating slope. Now it had all come to a sudden stop. As the wedding date grew closer and closer, the concept of spending the rest of his life with just one woman had increasingly frightened him. What if things didn't work out? What if he slid back to his old habits? He thought he loved Mary, but truth be known, he had no clear idea what love felt like since this would be his first time. So, when he added this uncertainty to the thought he might have to move to this land that God had forgotten, it scared the hell out of him.

The train whistle startled him. It was getting ready to pull out. He had the sensation that his lifeline was leaving, his last chance to escape was moving on.

He closed his eyes in one long blink and then opened them. The first sight he saw, outlined in one of the train windows, was an incredibly alluring woman with cascading black hair, olive dark skin, and almond shaped eyes. As he stared, she turned toward him, and smiled.

The next few moments were a blur, but as the train began to move, he found himself standing in the aisle of one of the passenger cars, right next to the window framed beauty.

Pulling his eyes from her, he watched the station gradually disappear as the train picked up speed. His first sensation was one of freedom, of euphoria. He'd escaped, he'd flown the cage, and he'd left a life of confinement behind him. And then the realization of what else he had left behind hit him. Panicked, he glanced around for the exit. It wasn't too late. He could jump off, and maybe even get back to the platform before Mary returned. As he took a step toward the exit, a sexy, husky voice halted his movement.

"Are you going in my direction?"

Sam stared back at the exotic beauty seated against the window. She was even more gorgeous than he'd expected. Somehow she seemed familiar, yet he knew he'd never met her because this type of woman would be etched into your permanent memory.

Almost against his will, he walked back toward her and said, "And what direction is that?"

She gestured out the window at the passing prairie. "Anywhere but here."

He nodded, staring out the window. "I was having the same thoughts." And as he spoke, he realized the train had picked up too much speed for him to jump off.

Don't panic, he told himself. I'll call Mary and explain. And then he remembered she had his cell phone and it was dying. Okay, I'll get off at the next stop and catch a ride back. This is merely a case of pre-wedding jitters. Mary will understand. But beneath this concern, he felt a sense of freedom, of release, of starting a new adventure. He tried to ignore it, but he couldn't deny its presence.

He swung his gaze back to the woman. "You look familiar." It was like she was a composite of the best features of all the women he had dated in the past. But that just couldn't be.

She smiled. "Maybe we met in another life."

He felt his old dating banter coming alive. "It must have been a good one."

She laughed, and then patted the seat next to her. "Come, sit with me."

Thoughts of leaving the train slid away as he moved in next to her. He'd been with Mary so long that this directness surprised him. Mary, who had captured him by her innocence and her shyness, was the anti-thesis of this woman. But he remembered women like this from his dating past when relationships were superficial and filled with sexual innuendos, and now, apparently, he was back to that. But when he'd first met Mary, it had all been different.

He'd been driving home late in the evening after a long day at work. It was a winding, dark road with very few cars at that time of night. His mind had been somewhere else when he suddenly realized that the car in front of him had braked to a stop. Only by the grace of God and a quick swerve to the right was he able to avoid rear ending the vehicle.

As he tried to calm his adrenaline charged system, he saw the driver's door open and a young woman jump out. She immediately ran around to the front of her car.

What the hell, Sam thought. After a moment it became clear she wasn't coming back so he climbed out to see what was going on.

He found her kneeling by the side of a yellow dog stretched out on the road. She was stroking the dog, and murmuring softly to it. As he approached, she looked up and he realized she was crying.

"I didn't see him. He just jumped out in front of me." She looked back at the dog. "He's still alive, but he's hurt. Fairly bad, I think."

Sam knelt down next to her. "Let me take a look." He bent over the dog. "Hello, fella. What's going on here?" He let the dog smell his hand, and then softly ran his fingers over the dog's body, all the while speaking in a calming voice. Several times the dog tried to rise, and each time Sam quieted him back down. As he was running his hand over the dog's back left leg, it yelped and snapped at his hand.

"It's okay, boy. You're going to be fine," he said, stroking the dog's head. He noticed the dog had a collar with a license.

"His back leg may be broken. He'll need x-rays to find out."

The girl wiped at her tears. "I don't even know where a vet's office is, much less one that's open this late."

"Well, I do. So here's what we'll do. You pull your car off the road, and then help me get him into the back of my car since I have more room there than you do. You'll have to sit with him to keep him calm."

The girl glared at him. "I have a can of mace in my purse."

"You won't need it. He's seems pretty tame."

"I wasn't thinking of the dog."

Sam sat back on his heels. "Well, since its confession time, you should know that I am a convicted sex offender who drives around looking for women who have an injured dog and need a ride to the vet's office."

They stared at each other for a moment, and then the girl half-smiled. Up until then, all he'd noticed was a young woman in baggy pants and a sweatshirt, topped off with a baseball cap, blond ponytail, and thick-rimmed red glasses. The smile changed it all. Pretty white teeth with shapely lips were set amongst a lightly tanned, clear complexion. Her eyes, though hidden behind the lens, were a sparkling brown with golden flecks.

After parking her car, they delicately maneuvered the dog into the back of Sam's automobile. The girl climbed in and put the dog's head on her lap, stroking it softly.

As he started the car and pulled away, he said over his shoulder, "My name's Sam."

There was no reply for a moment, and then a gentle voice said, "I'm Mary".

"Nice to meet you. The dog has a collar. See if there is an owner's name on it," he said.

"I see a person's name and a phone number. It seems that the dog's name is Penguin."

At the mention of his name, the dog weakly wagged his tail looking up at Mary. "I am so sorry, Penguin. But we are going to get you better." She glanced up. "How far away is the vet's office? I hope he's not so old that he can't remember what he learned in vet school."

"We're here," Sam said as they turned into a small empty parking lot. The office was a compact, single story building with a Spanish flare, and a sign with the logo, "All Creatures Great and Small Veterinarian Office".

"I don't see any lights," Mary said

"Doesn't mean they're closed."

"I pray this guy isn't one of those money grabbing quacks."

"Aren't they all," Sam replied, getting out of the car. He opened the back door and leaned in, "By the way, let me fully introduce myself. I am the local money grabbing quack that owns this business."

Mary shook her head. "And you let me babble on, sticking both feet in my mouth?"

"Well, I was busy trying to remember what I had learned in vet school."

"Okay, you got me. I apologize. I am sure that you are an excellent vet."

Sam just stared at her and then made a come-on like gesture with his hand.

Mary shrugged her shoulders. "You want more?"

"Do you think?"

"I am sure you are not a money grubbing quack... or at least I hope you aren't. And you are not too young or too old. Well, I'm not sure about the too old..."

Sam held up his hands in a stop motion. "Enough. Let's get Penguin out before these apologies get even more brutal."

Together they carried Penguin up to the front door, which Sam quickly opened. It took an hour, but the x-rays showed no evidence of fracture. The eventual diagnosis was just multiple bruises.

Sam called Penguin's owner to let them know he had the dog and what had happened. After a long conversation, he hung up the phone.

"You don't look happy. What's wrong?" Mary asked.

"Penguin's present owner is an eighty-year old woman whose daughter stuck her with the dog and then moved to New York." He rubbed his face. "She can't take care of him. He keeps getting out of her backyard which was never designed to hold a dog."

"And?"

"She's sorry but she doesn't want the dog back, and she can't afford to pay the bill."

They both stared at Penguin who was laid out on a gurney, still sedated for the x-rays.

"So what will you do with him?"

Sam shrugged. "He's a great looking dog. I'll see if I can find someone to adopt him."

"Why don't you take him?"

"My life is too hectic for a responsibility like that."

"Well, I'll pay the bill," Mary said.

"No, that's on me." He paused for a moment. "Instead, how about dinner some night?"

Mary gave him a smile. "That would be nice, but I have to say no. I'm engaged."

The train shuttered as it ran over an old section of track. Sam refocused and found his attractive companion staring at him with surprise.

"What?" he said.

"Most men don't suddenly zone out while I'm talking to them," she said. "Where did you go?"

"No place important." He turned fully toward her. "So tell me about yourself." God, had he really said that? His one liners use to be right on the money, now here he was throwing Hail Mary's just hoping for a catch. I have been out of the dating game too long, he realized.

"Let's start with the basics. I'm Alana," she replied, sticking out a slim, bejeweled hand.

"I'm Sam," he said, shaking it. She held his a bit longer than an introduction entailed, and then slowly released it.

"I'm a city girl," she said softly. "I like the noise, the lights, the excitement, and its pace. I would shrivel up and die in towns like these."

"How about small vacation towns, like Santa Barbara or Carmel?"

"Do they have five- star restaurants? All night discos were Cristal is the house champagne? No, New York, Chicago, and Paris - those are my vacation towns."

What a contrast to Mary, he mused. She loved quaint out of the way places, and Carmel was her favorite. He remembered the first time he'd seen her in Carmel.

It was an early morning in September, about a month after their first meeting. Sam was in the Carmel Coffee House on Ocean, the town's main street. He was moving toward the door to leave when a familiar face stepped in.

"Mary, hello."

She stared at him for a moment and then recognition clicked in. "Sam, how are you?" There seemed to be genuine interest in her voice.

"I'm doing well. Drove up with a friend for the weekend."

"Me too. My fiancé and I came for a couple of days," she said. "Unfortunately, he had to leave early this morning to get back to work."

"That's a shame. What does he do?"

She hesitated for a moment. "He plays baseball for the San Francisco Giants."

"No kidding. I'm a baseball fan. What's his name?"

"Hardy Jackman."

"Whoa. He is one hell of a player. I can't believe he didn't make the all-star team this year."

"Well, neither could he, but it's not a contract year so he wasn't that upset."

They made small talk as Mary got her coffee. When they stepped out onto the sidewalk, Sam gestured down the street. "If you'd like to join us, we're going to take a walk on the beach. It's absolutely gorgeous this time of the morning."

She shook her head. "I don't want to impose on you and your date."

"Well, at least come say hello," Sam said guiding her with his hand.

Mary glanced around and then looked bewildered. "Where is she?"

"Look down," he said, pointing at the golden lab whose leash was tied to a post.

"Oh, my God. Is that Penguin?" She dropped to one knee and stroked his back.

"The one and only."

"I thought your life was too busy to have a dog?" she said looking up.

"Well, times change. Besides, no one I knew wanted a dog."

"And this is the friend you came up with?"

"No, she's still sleeping at the hotel. Probably won't be up before eleven if I know her." Once again, he gestured down the street. "So come walk with us. Besides, Penguin needs someone to throw his ball." He sighed. "Too bad, Hardy had to leave. He could have given Penguin a real workout with that throwing arm of his."

Mary grinned and stood up. "All right, let's take that walk."

If anything, Sam decided, his description of the beach had been an under-exaggeration. The rising sun had colored the clouds a soft pink, while the slight off shore wind had smoothed the ocean as it gently blew the spray off the top of deep blue waves. The sand was a brilliant white set against the bright green of the distant Pebble Beach golf course. The tide was low making it a wide flat area to walk.

Mary stopped at the top of the sand dune which led down onto the beach. "Look at all the dogs," she said.

"Carmel is a dog friendly beach so it's dog city here in the morning. Gives the dogs a chance to play with others, while the owners get to socialize."

"Sounds like you've been here before."

"It's my home away from home. I love it here." Sam bent and unleashed Penguin who immediately raced down the dune to the water's edge, while they slowly followed him. The temperature was perfect with just a slight early morning chill.

As they talked and walked along the shoreline, Sam repeatedly threw the ball for Penguin who never got enough. Finally, he turned to Mary and handed her the ball. "Here, I don't want to have all the fun."

She laughed, taking the ball. Her throw had almost twice the distance of his.

"Where'd you get that arm?" he said, dodging a pool of salt water.

"Played softball for ten years. All-conference in my last two years at college."

"And now you're engaged to a baseball player. Makes some kind of sense I guess."

"I was a color commentator for the girl's college softball play-offs. Hardy was there to support girl's baseball," she replied, stepping over some seaweed.

"If taking attractive TV sportscasters out helps support girl's baseball, sign me up." They walked a while and then Sam asked, "When is the wedding?"

"Early December."

"Where?"

"Hardy loves New York so we're doing it there."

"And the honeymoon?" I asked, picking up Penguin's ball and giving it one of my anemic tosses.

"Tahiti, specifically Bora Bora. We are going to stay in one of those thatched huts out on the water. I am really excited."

"Well, it sure won't be bore-a-bore-a."

She pushed him. "That was bad?"

"Hang with me for a while. They get worse."

They reached the end of the beach and started back. "So what have you been doing since I saw you last," Mary asked.

"Other than overcharging everyone, I have been doing a lot of pro-bono work for the SPCA… which I blame on you."

"Me?"

"While I was trying to find a home for Penguin, I spent a lot of time dealing with the SPCA. Turns out, there are a lot of Penguin's out there that need help. So now I am the unofficial vet for our SPCA, supplying free medical care."

"Sam, that's nice." She jumped back from a rivulet of sea water.

"Well, your 'money grubbing quack' comment got to me. So if you and Hardy ever decide you need a dog, I've got a few dozen litters you can choose from."

They walked back up Ocean finally stopping in front of Mary's hotel.

"I will probably never see you again," Sam said, "so I'll just say that I wish it had been me at that fateful baseball game. We would have been an interesting couple."

Mary smiled and kissed him on the cheek. "At least it wouldn't have been bore-a boring."

"So where is home, Sam?" Alana asked.

"Southern California."

"Along the coast I hope. The rest is just miles of strip mall."

"Well, I don't know if it's that bad, but yeah I'm just a couple of blocks from the beach."

"What do you do?"

"I'm a veterinarian, both large and small animals."

"I'm a cat person myself. I love their independence, their sleek glossy coats, and the way they slink when they walk."

"Interesting description."

She purred. "Just think of me as a big cat that needs the sensual hands of a large animal vet."

Sam laughed. "I think I'd have to put you in restraints before I could safely examine you."

"Now that sounds exciting." She stared at him for a beat, and then burst out laughing. "I love to play the vamp role. Some men are so intimidated that they can barely speak." She smiled. "How about we get a drink and something to eat?"

The jangle of the conductor's keys, as he passed by them, ignited the memory of that fateful late night call.

It was two weeks after Sam's trip to Carmel. While driving home from work, he liked to listen to sports talk radio. On the hourly news recap, a name caught his attention.

"It was reported today that in the early hours of the morning Hardy Jackman was arrested for driving under the influence in Phoenix. Neither he nor his lawyer are available for comment."

As he pulled into his driveway, Sam switched off the radio. He fleetingly thought of Mary and wondered what the effects of this would be on her, then passed it off. Pro athletes were always getting arrested for DUI's, intoxication in public, or whatever. It never seemed to hurt their careers, and they could easily afford the fines.

The jangle of the phone woke him at three am. He fumbled for the receiver, nearly dropping it. "Hello," he croaked, "this is Dr. Lakota."

There was silence on the phone line. "Hello. Is there anyone there?" Still nothing but silence. What the hell, he thought, slamming the phone down.

He was just settling back to sleep when the phone rang again. He grabbed the receiver. "If this is some kind of prank, you're going to be sorry."

"Sam?" asked a hesitant voice.

It took a moment. "Mary, is that you?"

"I'm sorry to call so late."

"No, it's not too late."

"Don't give me that. You told me you were a confirmed early-to-bed, early-to-rise advocate."

"Well, I was just about to rise. What's up?"

"Did you hear the news today about Hardy?"

"I did. Sorry to hear about it, but it will pass."

"Did you see the story on the TV?"

"No, I heard it on the radio. Why, what's the difference?"

"The difference is the TV ran the pictures of his arrest and the bimbo he was with."

Sam sat up in the bed, putting his back against the headboard. "I'm sure there is some innocent explanation."

"Not at one am with a girl that looks like that!"

"Maybe he was just giving her a ride home from a late night party."

Mary was quiet for a moment. "Slight problem. I saw her in a picture with Hardy a few weeks ago... in a different town. He tried to tell me she was a teammate's girlfriend, and that was all."

Sam said gently, "What can I do to help?"

"I want to go back to Carmel, walk on the beach, throw the ball for Penguin, and watch the sunset over drinks. Will you go with me... as a friend?" Her question was answered with silence. "Sam, are you still there?"

"Sorry. I was busy packing."

Sam followed Alana back to the dining car where the waiter seated them at a small window table. The brightly decorated car contrasted sharply with the drab scenery out the window. As they read the menu, Alana began raving about the New York restaurants she'd frequented. Despite having spent some time in New York, Sam had never heard of any of them.

"What I wouldn't give for a glass of Opus One and a rib eye steak at Jean Georges," she said.

"Where's that?"

"Trump's International Hotel. Absolutely pristine with a simple black and white decor. Well worth the price. Not like Masa's, where you may pay $500 for sushi. Now that's a joke."

She looked up from the menu. "What do you feel like?"

"I thought I'd start slow. Say a double Jack Daniels on the rocks."

She grinned. "So it's been one of those days."

"You wouldn't believe it if I told you."

Alana pointed at the menu. "Do you think their Porterhouse would be eatable or am I being too optimistic?"

The word Porterhouse brought Sam's mind back to Carmel when he and Mary had gone on the "friend" weekend.

"I think I'll have a porterhouse tonight," Sam said. "How about you? What sounds good?"

They were seated at an intimate table high above the Pacific Ocean at the Highlands Inn with just a hint of sun light remaining on the horizon.

"I don't eat meat. I'm a vegan."

"So you don't eat chicken or fish either? What's the rule? You don't eat anything with a face?"

"Something like that."

"Well, how about we share some escargot? I'll take the face and you can have the other end."

They had taken the coast route up from Los Angeles with Penguin in the back seat. The last ninety miles or so had been on Highway One which runs along the edge of the ocean. After some initial pleasantries, Mary had become silent, just staring out the window. He had tried to make conversation, but finally elected to listen to music. They were passing San Simeon where the newspaper tycoon Randolph Hearst had his estate, when Mary spoke.

"I came to Hearst castle once with Hardy."

"I've never taken the tour, but I've heard the place is incredible."

"It has a huge pool surrounded by Greek sculptures. Absolutely beautiful. We joked about sneaking back in and skinny dipping at night." She paused. "I wonder how many other women he took there?"

Sam tried to shift the conversation to less troublesome topics, but now that the dam of silence had broken, remembrances of her and Hardy came pouring out. And since they had shared numerous trips on this part of the coast, the memories were plentiful. Camping at Big Sur, lunch at Nepenthe, walking the driftwood strewn beaches. Gradually her tone changed from reflection to anger, and then to blame and question. Maybe it was her fault? Maybe she should have been more understanding of his job and the situations it might place him in? Maybe he had just been giving the girl a ride home? Maybe she was just another player's girlfriend? Had she been too quick to disbelieve him?

Sam attempted to answer, but soon realized she wasn't speaking to him but rather to herself, giving voice to her doubts and worries so she could review them and make conclusions.

They checked into their dog friendly hotel in the late afternoon, specifically into a one bedroom cottage down along the Carmel River. As they entered, Sam explained that Mary could have the bedroom while Penguin and he would take the couch in the living room. Her relief was obvious.

They drifted down to Carmel Beach to watch the sunset and it was spectacular. As it sank low on the horizon, Sam told her to watch for the "green flash."

"I thought that was folk lore?"

"Keep your eyes glued on the sun. Just as it disappears, you may see a flash of green. Lasts for just a few seconds, then gone."

She was quiet and then said, "Kind of like my relationship with Hardy."

He put his arm around her and gave her a slight shake. "Watch!"

And there it was, just for a fleeting moment, but clear as could be, a momentary pulse of green.

"Oh, my God. It really does exist," Mary said.

"That is nature's way of telling you that you have a green light to move on with your life and quit doubting yourself."

It was late when they finally got back from dinner, and both of them were tired from the long drive. Mary headed for the bedroom, and stopped at the door. "Thank you so much. This really has been a nice day, and you've been so great putting up with my whining and complaining."

"Think nothing of it. I never heard a thing. It's was a pleasure to be with you." He paused, and then put his hands out in a question. "Did I overdo that?"

She laughed. "No, it sounded very sincere." She turned to go into the room, and paused. "I'm still a bit shook up about

Hardy. I would love to have someone cuddle with me in bed," she said in an alluring, sexy voice.

Sam was just stepping forward, when she added, "Come on, Penguin".

Alana leaned back in her chair and pushed her plate away. "Surprisingly, that was not bad." She looked about for the waiter. "I'm going to have an after dinner drink. What about you?"

Moving his plate aside, Sam said, "I don't seem to have an appetite, but I could use another drink."

"How about a couple of tequila shooters?" she asked mischievously.

Sam blanched as his stomach turned over, and he quickly shook his head. "Anything but that." In his mind baseball and tequila were forever entwined since that Carmel trip.

Sam and Mary were up early the next day, breakfasting on coffee and scones. Later, a walk on the beach with Penguin, a hike around Point Lobos state park, and finally dinner. As the day had progressed, Mary's comments about her life with Hardy had faded. The sunlight, the quaint town of Carmel, the sensational beaches, and the startling greens of the Pebble Beach golf courses would have make anyone perk up, and it had that effect on Mary. By dinner time, they had developed a comfortableness around each other that let them slide easily into discussions of their hopes, their dreams, their successes, and their failures, both in business and relationships. They laughed, they groaned, they commiserated as the conversation wandered over the peaks and valleys of their lives. Sam had never felt so unguarded, so open to talking about his personal life. As the night wore on, he realized that Mary's real beauty was her inner person. Everything he learned about her just entranced him even more.

Afterwards, they stopped into a small sports bar for a nightcap. While they were waiting for their drinks, they realized the TV was tuned to the Giants baseball game. Apparently they were playing their longtime rival, the Dodger's. The noise in the bar immediately picked up as the game resumed.

Sam glanced at Mary who was staring at the screen. "Do you want to leave? There are a lot of other places we can go."

She shook her head. "I have to learn how to handle this since it's going to come up over and over."

Sam thought for a moment. "Then why don't we make it a fun learning experience? Every time Hardy comes to bat and gets on base, you have to take a shot. Every time he fails to get on base, I take a shot."

Mary laughed. "I can do that. So what are we drinking? Shots of tequila?"

"Fine by me."

The next morning, Sam slowly opened his eyes. Just that motion alone caused an explosion in the back of his head. Gradually, the room came into focus and he realized he wasn't on the couch but rather in the bed. And at that moment of comprehension, he felt movement next to him. Oh, God, what have I done he thought. He'd meant to be a gentleman this weekend, and not take advantage of this wonderful girl in distress, especially since he felt so strongly about her.

He started rolling over. "I am so sorry. I never meant this to…" And came face to face with Penguin.

There was a knock on the door. "Hey in there. Are you decent? I have fresh coffee."

Sam eased himself upright, ran his hand through his hair which did nothing but aggravate his headache, and tried again to clear his vision. "Yeah, come on in," he croaked.

Mary entered carrying a tray of muffins and coffee. "Glad to see you're back with the living."

After he'd drunk half a cup and decided he wasn't going to die after all, Sam said, "How did I end up in the bed?"

"Well, you were in no shape to sleep on the couch. In fact, you were in no shape at all. I had to have the cab driver help me get you into the bedroom."

"What happened last night?"

"Well, the game went extra innings so Hardy came up to bat six times and... never got on base."

Sam groaned. "Never got on base? Not even a walk?"

Mary looked away. "Did I...ah... mention he was in a bad slump?

"No, I think you left that fact out." He paused. "Anything else I should know about last night."

"Well, I tried several times to get you to leave the bar, but you were adamant about staying. You eventually offered to buy everyone a drink."

"Oh, great. How much did that cost me?"

"Not much. By then, we were the only ones left. In fact, they were closing up around us."

Sam hung his head. "I am really sorry if I embarrassed you there."

"Oh, that was nothing. The embarrassment came when we got here. As the cabby was helping me move you into the cottage, you kept shouting over and over, 'Be gentle with me. I'm a virgin'. Woke the whole compound up."

Later that morning, they drove south. It was Sam's turn to be quiet on the ride back to LA. Several times nausea forced him to stop but he never threw up. Mary did all the talking, and laughing about the weekend while he feebly tried to keep up his end of the conversation. She was clearly out of the funk she had been in on the drive up. Sam drove to her apartment.

"No need for you to get out," Mary said as she opened her car door.

"Are you afraid I might embarrass you again?"

She laughed. "I had a really, really nice time. This weekend was exactly what I needed."

Sam stared at her for along moment.

"What?" she said.

"Some more weekends with you is exactly what I need," he replied.

After a momentary pause, she leaned in and kissed him on the cheek. "I think that can be arranged."

And so their relationship started and blossomed over the next year and a half, until one day it was the most natural thing for Sam to ask for her hand in marriage, which then eventually led to their trip to the lovely town of River Bottom.

Sipping on an Irish coffee, Sam stared across the table at Alana. She was gorgeous, entertaining, and… not Mary. That was the problem. No one else was Mary. No one was going to fill her place. No one had her grace, her humor, her compassion, her ability to make him feel so in touch with the excitement of living. He understood now that any other woman would just be a runner-up wife, not the first place one he'd just abandoned.

"You look like you made a decision," Alana said setting her glass of wine down.

"I have made a major mistake that I can only hope to rectify."

At that instant the train began to slow. Sam glanced out the window. He could see buildings, probably the outskirts of a town. He stood up, dropped some money on the table, and said, "Have a nice life. This is where I get off."

Alana ran her finger around the top of her glass. "I hope she's worth it."

"No, I hope I am worthy of her." And then he was down the aisle, and jumping off the train as it slowly pulled into the station. He had no idea where he was and there were no signs to help. Quickly he walked to the ticket window, only to discover it was closed. A schedule posted next to the window listed the next train heading back toward River Bottom wouldn't be passing through for another 24 hours.

Sam turned away and walked back to the platform staring at the train. Alana was framed in the window, regarding him with a slight smile.

"Oh God, what have I done," Sam said out loud. He closed his eyes, hearing the conductor telling everyone to get aboard, smelling the exhaust of the engine, and faintly tasting the rusting steel of the cars. He opened his eyes again, still seeing Alana in the window, only now there was no desire to escape or enticement to go after her, but rather just a hollowness.

He felt a hand on his shoulder. Turning, he saw Mary standing next to him. Shocked, he started to speak, but she spoke first. "My parents will be here in twenty minutes. They are so excited to meet you."

Glancing around, Sam saw the faded "River Bottom, Kansas" sign on the station wall, and saw the same group of aged buildings that made up the town he thought he'd left. He was still in River Bottom. He had never left. This had all just been his imagination… or had it? He turned back to the train which was just pulling out. Sitting in the dining car, Alana lifted her glass of wine, smiled back at him, and then was gone as the train rolled by.

"Who was that woman?" Mary asked.

It was then that the realization hit him. "She was my past," he said slowly.

"What..."

Sam grabbed her, cutting off her question, and hugged her to his chest.

Mary gently pushed him away. "Enough, big guy. You're crushing me."

Sam flung his arm out to encompass the station, the town, and the surrounding barren plains. "I love it here," he said in a loud and excited voice. "I want to live here with you for the rest of my life."

Mary stepped back, giving him a wide eyed appraisal. "You would live here?"

"I want to live where you want to live. So if we have the time, let's check out the real estate market, see if there are any homes we might like."

"Well if you find a home you like, you will be living here alone. I have no plans to spend the rest of my life in this dust bowl. A visit here once every few years is all I can handle."

* * * * *

Author's Note: I have always been amazed at how quickly life can change. One minute you are driving down the street heading for a party, and the next someone hits your car and you are paralyzed for life. In those few seconds, life is irreversibly changed and you have nothing to say about it. The alterations may be major, such as being fired from a job or your spouse leaving you. They can also be catastrophic, such as sudden loss of vision. But the point is that in that blink of an eye, your whole life has irrevocably changed.

So I wondered what if you make a sudden decision in your life, only to realize it was the wrong choice, and then it all changed back. How might that affect your outlook? Would the complaints of your present life still seem as distasteful or would you evaluate them in a different light?

I lived in Manhattan Beach in Southern California for a number of years, and then Carmel for much longer, so those locations formed the backdrop for the story. And as a man born and raised on the edge of the ocean, I, like Sam, would have had a difficult adjustment moving away from it.

Hemingway's Whiskey

My wife says it was just one of those nights, but I wouldn't call partying with a ghost, somersaults off the bar, indiscriminately kissing random women, and ravishing the lead singer just one of those nights. I blame it on the liquor, and if truth be told, so does she. After all, what else would you expect drinking Hemingway's Whiskey.

It was five years ago, but I remember it like it was yesterday. I had been recently dumped by my longtime girlfriend, and was wallowing in self-pity. Hoping to work my way out of that, I had relocated to Key West with some vague thought of searching for my inner self or finding a new girlfriend or whatever. Unfortunately, finding anything was hard to do when you slept all day, and worked all night. That wouldn't have been bad if I'd worked in a bar and could have had a social life, but no, the only job I could find was working at night in the Hemingway Heritage House as a house painter with one other social misfit.

The curator had wanted the whole inside painted, but didn't want that to interfere with the tourists traffic during the day, so the solution was painting at night. For the last four nights I had worked alone since my sole companion had broken his arm skateboarding to work.

The evening in question started out as usual with me setting up my painting utensils and ladders. After about three hours of slapping paint on walls, I realized I needed a break or I was going to fall asleep standing up. At the time, I was just outside the master bedroom and its double bed had beckoned until I couldn't fight the call. Stretching out, I promised myself I'd just close my eyes for a few minutes and then get back to work.

It was the voice that woke me - "What the hell are you doing in my bed?" - a strong, boisterous voice, not what I would have expected coming from the dead man standing at the foot of my bed. And, as far as I knew, Ernest Hemingway had been dead for a lot of years.

I should have been scared to death, with a pounding heart, shaking limbs, and quivering voice. Instead I just stared. This had to be a dream. I'd been in Hemingway's house for the last two weeks and avidly caught up in its history, so it was natural that I might dream about him. That had to be the answer.

I sat up, swung my legs over the side of the bed, and rubbed my eyes figuring that would wake me. But when I stopped rubbing, the apparition still remained, his eyes radiating hostility. He was tall with a moderate girth, grey hair, a short white beard, and dressed in a safari jacket. Yep, he looked like all the pictures I'd seen of Hemingway in his later years. All he lacked was a glass of liquor or a deep sea fishing rod. I was surprised my dream hadn't added one or both of those accessories.

"I asked you a question," the man or spirit said aggressively.

"The Hemingway estate hired me to paint the interior of this house."

"Still doesn't answer my question."

"Didn't get much sleep yesterday so I was just taking a cat nap."

He harrumphed. "The only cats that get to nap around here have six toes." He pointed at my bare feet. "You don't qualify."

I knew the stories about Hemingway's six-toed cats. "It was just a figure of speech," I explained.

He stared at me for nearly a minute and then seemed to come to some peaceful resolution. Glancing around the large, high ceilinged room with its wainscoting and French doors opening on to the balcony, he said, "Hasn't changed much since I was last here." He glanced over at me. "Do you imbibe?"

"Who are you?"

"Who the hell do you think I am, you trespasser?" That peaceful mental resolution of his was shaking loose.

I softened my tone. "Well you look like Hemingway, but he's dead."

"Well, you are right on both counts."

As if that answered it all, he turned and walked over to a far wall. Hitting it with the palm of his hand, a small door swung open. He reached in and removed a nearly full bottle of liquor and two thick glasses.

A half-smile flittered quickly across his face and then it was gone. "You'll join me, of course." The intimidation in his eyes left little choice. He used his foot to push a small wooden chest over to the bed and set the bottle and glasses on it. Grabbing a chair, he joined me at the make shift table and started to pour.

"Make mine small," I said. "I still have to work tonight." Even in my dream, I managed to keep some semblance of a work ethic.

Stopping in mid-pour, he looked over at me with disgust. "If you're drinking with me, you drink like a man." He filled each glass about half way, and handed one to me. Lifting his glass in a toast, he said staring at me, "To quick hands in the ring, a strong line on the pole, and a pretty woman always at your table." With that, he emptied his glass and then banged it down on the chest.

"Ahhhh," he said, almost like a post-coital exclamation. Picking the empty glass back up, he stared at it in the glare of the overhead light. "ALMOST, and that's in capital letters, almost forgot how good that tastes."

He pointed at my untouched glass. "It's considered an insult not to match your host in drinking."

What the hell, I thought. This is only a dream, so I drank it all down. And if this isn't a dream, I realized, I had just kissed off getting any work done tonight. Surprisingly, the liquor was very tasty.

"What is this?" I asked, pointing at the bottle.

"It's my own brand of scotch. I call it, modestly of course, Hemingway's Whiskey."

Before I could protest, my host had filled both our glasses again. At this rate, I might not get any work done tomorrow night either. And then it hit me who this guy was.

"You're here for the Hemingway look-a-like contest, aren't you?"

"What are you talking about, son?"

"Each year, Sloppy Joe's bar puts on a Hemingway look-a-like contest and its being held this week." I saw his confusion and pressed on. "And that's how you ended up here in Hemingway's old estate. Right?"

He put back his head and emitted a deep, roaring laugh. "I can't believe it. After all these years, Sloppy's still exists. It's my favorite watering hole. In fact I supplied Joe with some of the money to buy it."

"Well, it's still there and doing big business."

"And you're telling me they have a contest each year to see who looks the most like me? That's ridiculous. I didn't even want to look like me."

This had continued long enough. "So who are you if not a Hemingway impersonator?"

"I am Ernest Hemingway and this was my home with my second wife, Pauline. That was our wedding bed you just desecrated."

Yep, this dream was only getting weirder, but I might as well go with it. "Well, I'm sorry to inform you, but you are dead. You committed suicide with a shotgun in 1961."

He shook his head. "It wasn't suicide. I was cleaning the damn gun. It was supposed to be unloaded." He paused. "Unfortunately, I was loaded." Once again, the roaring laugh.

"Whatever, you're still dead. Am I just supposed to believe you are a ghost?"

"Believe what you want, but the fact is that I am Hemingway, and I'm back."

I thought for a moment. "Back for what? In all the ghost stories I've heard of, spirits usually come back for a purpose."

"Great question." He paused and then said, "Truth is that I have no idea why I'm here at this particular time and place." He looked me over and then groaned. "God, I hope it's not just to meet you."

"Ha, ha," I said sarcastically. "So where have you been all these years?"

He gazed off in the distance, and then said uncertainly, "Not sure. All I remember is vague shadows, and strange forms."

We stared at each other, and I could see the puzzlement in his face. I would have been feeling the same way if I had been brought back to life only to be thrust into an empty house with a depressed painter. "Maybe I will have another drink," I said. Seems that even in my dream, I needed alcohol to confront all this.

He poured two. After a quick gulp of his, he said resignedly, "So what the hell? If I'm here for some reason, it will become clear. In the meantime, how about we head down to Sloppy's for a round or two?"

It was apparent that work was not going to play a role in this dream. "Sounds good to me," I said. "And by the way," I added, sticking out my hand, "I'm Charley Stone." We shook. I slipped on my socks and shoes, and we went downstairs and out the side gate.

We continued through the alley for half a block and then turned left onto Duval Street. I knew that Sloppy Joe's was six or seven blocks down.

The sidewalks were packed with people, as were the restaurants.

"Is there some special event going on tonight?" Hemingway asked. "I've never seen so many people on the streets before."

I laughed. "This is a slow night. On the weekends we would have trouble even making our way through the hordes."

After examining this passing flow of humanity, Hemingway said, "What is it with the piercings on the men? In my day, earrings on a male meant they had sailed around one of the Horns. Some of these guys don't look like they could walk around a corner."

"It's the in-thing." I saw his confusion at my word choice. "It's a popular fashion."

As we made our way along Duval Street, he continued his scrutiny of the passing crowds, occasionally shaking his head at some of the sights. "How long have you been in the Keys?" he asked while still keeping up his rubbernecking.

"Moved down a few months ago."

"Why down here?"

"It's a long story."

"Make it a short one."

"Longstanding girlfriend dropped me for another because she claimed I was too boring. She wanted, and I quote 'a wild man'."

We stepped around a couple on the sidewalk that should have been getting a room.

"Was she right?" he asked.

Reluctantly, I nodded. "I guess I had lost sight of how to have fun. But I was busy trying to…" My words trailed off.

"Busy doing what?" He glanced at me and then laughed. "Don't tell me you're a writer."

"Well, I'm trying to be."

"And what are you writing about?"

"It's a slice of life story but it's just flat. My ex claims it's because boring can only write about boring." I paused. "I thought moving down here would change that. Surrounded by so many creative people in this low key environment, I hoped to come alive emotionally and creatively. Instead, I paint bland walls with bland paint."

Hemingway threw his arm around me. "Charley, you do have to experience life to write about it." With a chuckle, he added, "Most of my books were essentially autobiographical. I just changed the names."

"Easy for you. Your life filled books, while my life lately is a short chapter."

"Then tonight we get some more chapters for your book. And Sloppy's is just the place to start."

Sloppy Joe's was on the corner of Greene and Duval. The outside looked fairly up to date, but the inside was another story. It was basically a large square room with a high ceiling, worn wood walls, multiple well used bars, and a large raised stage against the back wall. Memorabilia lined the walls, with stuffed fish, Hemingway pictures, historical photographs of the area, and other bric-a-brac. The place was packed, but as we entered two barstools became available. We were near the front of the room at a U-shaped bar that let us look across the other side of the bar to the stage. After we settled in, I pointed out the banner above the stage. "Hemingway Look-A-Like Contest. Preliminaries Thursday and Friday. Finals Saturday."

The bartender slid up and tossed a few napkins down. "What are you having, gents?"

"Two scotch and waters," Hemingway said.

Staring at my companion, the bartender said, "See you're here for the contest."

"What are his chances," I said with a grin.

After a quick scrutiny, the bartender replied, "So, so. There are some real dead-ringers this year." He thought for a moment, and then added, "But with some additional weight, more white in the hair and beard, and a stronger speaking voice, you might have a chance."

I slapped Hemingway on the back. "Better luck next year."

"Is Joe Russell or Big Skinner still around?" Hemingway asked.

The bartender gave him a quizzical look, and then said, "Man, you are really getting into the part. Those two have been dead for what... 40 years? Most of these look-a-likes don't even know who they were." He smiled and turned to leave. "Be right back with your drinks."

I could see that Hemingway had taken the news hard. "Hey, maybe they'll show up as ghosts and join us." His glare cut me to the core so I turned to watch the action on the stage. The band had just come on and was tuning their instruments. There was a lead guitarist, bass guitarist, drummer, and a female vocalist. She had long black hair in ringlets, lots of dark eye makeup, white shirt with the ends tied into a knot just under her breasts exposing a taught stomach. Short shorts with cowboy boots completed the outfit. Lots of silver jewelry and a left arm with a sleeve of colored tattoos. On the base drum was written, "Cat Black and the Midnight Howlers."

"Attractive woman despite the outfit," Hemingway said just as the bartender arrived. He set our drinks down and left. I took a sip of mine and nearly spit it out. This tasted nothing like what we'd had at the house. Seeing my revulsion, Hemingway took my glass and drank it down. He then pulled a flask from his back pocket, filled my tumbler, and handed it back to me. "Try this," he said.

It was exactly what we'd been drinking before. I normally wasn't a scotch drinker, but this Hemingway's Whiskey was delicious.

Hemingway pointed at the bar tab.

"Don't tell me" I said cutting him off, "you don't have any money, so this dream is on me."

"I'll get the next round," he offered with a Cheshire cat smile.

The band started up, and the first song was actually very good. I realized immediately, that Cat Black was the show. She had a smoky, sensual voice that was the perfect accompaniment to her sexy, erotic gyrations on the stage. If you were a man with even the barest level of testosterone, you couldn't fail to be wowed.

The next song was also nicely done with good instrumentation that went well with her voice. Immediately, couples got up and started dancing. As the music rolled on, Hemingway leaned in to me. "Time to dive into the river of humanity and get some memories."

"What?"

"Go ask someone to dance." He saw my hesitancy, and his eyebrows arched in surprise. "You can dance, can't you?"

The old me would have sat and watched, but with the alcohol, his urging, and knowing this was only a dream, I went in search of a partner. I had seen one young woman dance earlier, and she could move. I found her standing with several of her friends.

"Would you like to dance?" I said.

She looked me up and down, and obviously wasn't impressed with my wrinkled, paint stained work clothes. "Thank you, but I'm sitting this one out."

Instead of falling into my usual retreat mode, I pressed on. "Don't let the exterior fool you."

The next song started and it was fast with a great beat.

Putting my hands out to her, I said, "East coast or west coast swing?"

That caught her attention, so I followed it up. "Make you a deal. If I don't dance your socks off, I'll cover your bar bill for the night."

She smiled. "And if you do knock them off…?"

"A kiss at the end of the dance."

Her girlfriends pushed her toward me. "Do it, Jane. Think of the free drinks."

As I spun my new partner on to the floor, I whispered a "Thank you, mom," referring to the years of endless dance lessons my mom had forced on me.

We were cautious at first, making a few thrusts and parries to get a better feel for each other. And then we got to it, making move after move, some of which I hadn't tried for years. But everything was working. We danced like we had practiced together for years. She was an excellent dancer and had no problem following my lead. Slowly the other couples stepped back to watch, and even I was amazed with our natural choreography. Was it the alcohol, a great dance partner, or reckless abandonment? Who cared? It was a blast and I didn't know why I hadn't done this years ago. When the song ended, we not only got applause from the other couples but also from the band. When I looked up to acknowledge them, Cat Black winked at me.

As I walked Jane back to her friends, I pointed down to her feet. "I think your socks are missing."

She was momentarily confused and then laughed.

"A bet is a bet," I said smiling as I puckered up, and leaned forward.

Viewing my ridiculous pose, she exclaimed, "Oh, be still my trembling heart," then bent forward and kissed me on the cheek.

"Well aren't you a regular Fred Astaire," Hemingway said with a wiry grin as I rejoined him.

I saw three empty glasses in front of him. "I see someone is making up for lost time." I grabbed one of the glasses and pushed it toward him. "Anything left in that flask of yours?"

As he was pouring, someone tapped me on the shoulder. It was a cute, mildly overweight, young woman. "Would you like to dance?" she said hesitantly.

My initial reaction was to slide back into my sideline shell and politely refuse, but Hemingway elbowed me off the stool and said, "He'd love to."

My new dance partner was not as accomplished as my previous one, but she could follow and together we did a bang-up job. She had a great sense of humor, and we stayed on the floor for another dance, laughing and joking. As I left the dance floor, three girls stopped me, and each asked me to dance.

With my shell now shattered, I was ready for anything. Instead of choosing just one, I invited them all out on to the floor but warned them that I required a kiss from each at the close of the song.

My dance steps were tremendously ad lib but I kept all three girls busy with move after move. They were sharp enough to throw a few improvisations in themselves, and we basically took over the dance floor. People in the surrounding tables were clapping to the music and cheering us on… as if we needed encouragement. As the song neared its end, I maneuvered the girls into a half circle. While they continued to dance, I jumped up on a chair, and stepped onto the bar. Turning quickly, I did a somersault, landing in front of the girls where I dropped to my knees just as the song ended. The place went crazy. Applause, shrieks, and shouts of more. The girls and I took a bow, and I got a peck on the cheek from each of them. On my way back to the bar, one of the bouncers pulled me aside.

"Love the moves," he said, "but stay off the bar."

When I reached my bar stool, Hemingway was gone. I caught the bartender's attention. "Have you seen my friend?"

He pointed to one of the smaller bars on the other side of the room. I saw him standing in discussion with a number of the Hemingway look-a-likes. The bartender leaned in and said, "He said to put all his drinks on your tab."

"No problem."

"Just so you know, he's been buying drinks for the whole group over there."

I started to protest, and then realized this was merely a dream so what the hell. He could buy the whole place drinks for all I cared.

There was a tap on my back. "I'm sorry," I said over my shoulder, "but I'm sitting this one out."

"Well, I am too, cowboy." And Cat Black hopped up on the stool next to me.

We stared at each other for a long moment, and I finally stammered out a response. "Nice sounds."

She smiled. "Nice dancing."

Well, I could do the compliment game. "Nice outfit."

"Not as distinctive as yours." Gesturing to my overalls and black T-shirt, both covered with paint splotches, she asked, "Your own design?"

"Cross between Farmers' Almanac and House Painter's Guide." I pointed at her left arm, covered with an intricate, multi-color-ed tattoo. "Your design?"

Lifting her arm, she examined it, twisting it back and forth. "No, it was just handy at the time." She grinned, leaned in, and said softly, "It's not real. Just need to keep up the image."

I laughed. "You mean you aren't really an edgy, multi-pierced, rock star existing on drugs and alcohol?"

"Oh, I am all those things, but the tattoo is fake."

The bartender set a glass in front of her with ice and some brown liquid. I'd seen her sipping the same thing up on the stage.

"What are you drinking?" I asked.

"Have a sip."

It was root beer. "You and Dean Martin," I said. "Supposedly he didn't really drink when performing."

"You can't. It ruins your timing. These people came to see a good show, not some drunken girl on a stage."

"Well, you give a great performance."

"I haven't seen you in here before," she said taking a sip from her drink.

"I work nights." I spread out my arms to show my outfit more clearly. "Painting."

"So on your night off, you dress in your work clothes?"

"No, I got pulled away from work." I took a sip of my whiskey. "I'm here with a guy that thinks he's Hemingway's ghost."

She gave me a skeptical look, but before she could speak I said, "No, he's not a look-a-like, he thinks he is the real thing."

Shrugging her shoulders, she said, "It takes all kinds, but at least its novel."

I noticed that the band had re-assembled and was getting ready to play. "Aren't you supposed to be up there?" I said, pointing toward the stage.

"No, each night I let Jason - our lead guitarist - do a few songs on his own. He's got a good voice, but not enough to carry the band alone."

"I noticed that you two seemed pretty tight on the stage. Are you guys an item?"

"An item? Who talks like that?" She giggled. "We are like brother and sister, especially since he's gay."

The music had started and Jason wasn't bad, but not in Cat's caliber.

"So, are you going to ask me to dance or what?" she said. Seeing my surprise, she added, "I hope you don't think I came over just to admire your outfit."

I popped off my bar stool, turned, and offered my hand. "I'm ready when you are.

"I need a little something to oil my joints," she said, grabbing my half-full glass and drinking it down. She looked at the empty glass, then at me. "That was delicious. What is it?"

"Hemingway's Whiskey. And you know what they say about whiskey," I replied, raising my eyebrows several times, and then we both chimed in together. "It's whiskey that makes you frisky."

With that we were out on the dance floor. I spun her once and immediately knew she was a dancer. The band must have seen us because the music got louder, and the beat more pounding. My previous trips to the dance floor had just been a warm up for what we were doing now. Everything I tried, she knew and did it better than anyone I had ever danced with before. Then she started showing me moves I had never seen, but since I'm a quick learner, we were off and doing it all. Slowly the floor cleared and it was just us, each pushing the other.

I spun her off, but instead of coming back, she hopped up on the bar and beckoned me to join her. I looked over at the bouncer who shrugged his shoulders, and then gave me a nod. In no time, I was up there with her and we were rocking, and we were rolling. Anything left on the bar was fair game, and Cat downed three beers and one mixed drink before people yanked their drinks back protectively off the bar. Once again, people were clapping and shouting as we boogied down the length of the bar and back. As the music hit its closing crescendo, I leaped off the bar, turning 180 degrees, so when I landed I was facing Cat. Almost immediately, she sprang off and I caught her in my outstretched arms just as the song ended.

I was off balance, though, when she landed and it sent me staggering backwards. Totally losing it, I fell back against a wall and slid to the floor, with Cat landing in my lap. We stared at each other for a moment, and then both of us burst out laughing. As the band started their next song, the dance floor filled, and we were no longer the center of attention.

"You are one hell of a dancer," I said. "I could barely keep up with you."

"You aren't so bad, yourself, cowboy."

"Where did you learn to dance?" I said.

"I minored in college in both dance and music."

Shaking my head in wonder, I said, "I haven't had that much

fun for a long time. I wish this wasn't just a dream."

"A dream?"

"I am partying with Hemingway's ghost and dancing with the most beautiful lady in the bar. What else could this be but a dream?"

She gave me a long stare, and I found myself caught up in the dark brown of her eyes. "Time for a wake-up call, cowboy," she said, and kissed me. It started out as a friendly peck, but then somehow it evolved into a barnburner. When we came up for air, I let out a loud, "Whoa. Now that was a kiss."

Giving me her sexiest stare, she said, "Still think this is a dream?"

"I am making out with the hottest girl in the bar, so yes this definitely fills all official criteria for a dream."

She grinned and then looked perplexed. "You know, that's the first time I've ever kissed someone in a bar, much less at one of my shows. How strange."

"Join the crowd. That's the first time I've ever danced on a bar or with more than one lady at a time."

"So we're both acting a bit crazy. What's going on here?"

We stared at each other for several moments, and then I said, "Hemingway's Whiskey!" Cat frowned so I explained. "Ever since I had my first drink, I haven't been acting like myself. And you had a pretty good sized gulp of that right before we started dancing."

"Charley Stone, is that you?" a female voice asked.

We both looked up and there stood Daphne, my ex-girlfriend, with a shocked expression.

Just yesterday, if Daphne had spoken to me I would have leaped to my feet, full of embarrassment for what I'd just done. But that was yesterday. Now, I felt very comfortable remaining on the floor, leaning against the wall, with Cat in my lap.

"Daphne! What are you doing in my dream?" I said with surprise and regret.

She gave me a quizzical look, and then said, "I'm here on vacation with a few of my girlfriends, when one of them says, 'Isn't that Charlie dancing on the bar?'" Her eyes widened with the memory. "I told them of course not. I don't think he even knows how to dance. And then I knew it couldn't be you when I saw you groveling on the floor with…" she pointed at Cat, "this whatever she is. My God, what's happen to you?"

I felt Cat start to move and I held her down. "Cat, this is Daphne, my ex-girlfriend. And Daphne, this is Cat, the lead singer for the band. If you have anything more to say about her, please keep it to yourself."

Cat glanced up at her and I could see the mischief forming in her eyes. "Nice to meet you, Daffy." Cat then turned to me, and said, "Now where were we? Oh, yeah." With that, she pulled me to her and started to kiss me, climbing all over me as she did, until I ended up flat on the floor with Cat laying on top of me. It was no surprise when we finished that Daphne was long gone. I believe I heard a "You're disgusting" or something like that just before she left.

Cat climbed off of me, and leaned back up against the wall. "You use to go out with her?" The disbelief was heavy in her voice.

"We broke up five months ago." My tone must have expressed more than my words, for her next question was in a softer, gentler tone.

"What happened? Other than you woke up and realized she wasn't the girl for you."

"Hey, I was thinking of marrying her until she dumped me for some stockbroker cash-hole."

She reached into her back pocket and gave me a five dollar bill.

"What's that for?" I said.

"To buy the guy a thank you card," she said with a straight face which lasted no more than five seconds before she erupted with laughter. I joined in and it felt good because now I knew Daphne was definitely out of my system. I stood and helped Cat get up.

"I need to get back to the band," she said.

"Not before you meet my ghost friend," I said pulling her toward the secondary bar on the far side of the room.

We made our way through the crowd, and finally found Hemingway surrounded by a bunch of look-a-likes. They were in a heavy discussion about the real Hemingway's past history.

"He was married four times not three," one of the look-a-likes said.

"You gentlemen call yourself Hemingway look-a-likes, and yet don't know the details of his life?" Hemingway asked in shock.

"Hey, in this contest it's more important to look like him than know about him."

Hemingway thought about that for a moment. "Maybe the most important thing is to drink like him," he said with a roar. "Another round of drinks on me, Jake." They all moved over to the bar.

"Sure thing, Mr. Hemingway," Jake the bartender replied, as he began lining up the glasses.

"So you're actually related to the real Hemingway," a look-a-like said.

"I'm as closely related as humanly possible," Hemingway replied with a grin. "Ask me anything about him."

"What did he like to drink?" someone said.

"Anything in a bottle if push came to shove. But he favored scotch and soda, gimlets, champagne, and of course, an occasional martini."

"Is it true that after he died, when they opened his safe, there was a picture of that nurse he fell in love with in Italy? I can't remember her name," another look-a-like said.

Hemingway went silent, so after a few moments, I stepped in. "Her name was Agnes von Kurowsky, and yes the story is true."

I glanced over at Hemingway, and he was glaring at me. What the hell, I thought, the truth is the truth. "They fell in love while he was hospitalized in Italy. She was supposed to follow him over, but several months after he arrived in the states, she wrote…"

Hemingway cut me off. "That she had become engaged to an Italian army officer." He tossed back the drink he was holding, and then called to the bartender. "Jake, another please."

"He was devastated by her rejection," I said. "Word has it she was the model for the nurse in Farewell to Arms, and he killed her off in the end to get even."

Cat grabbed my arm and pulled me aside. "What was that name you just mentioned?"

"Agnes von Kurowsky. Why?"

"That was my great grandmother." She saw my surprise. "What did she have to do with Hemingway?"

I explained the connection, and then added, "She was pivotal in his life. Her abandonment, historians think, is why Hemingway's life followed a pattern of abandoning each of his wives before they could desert him. Hence the four wives in forty years."

"Oh, my God," Cat said. "That is not the way it happened. She didn't abandon him. It was all a mistake."

I was shouldered aside as Hemingway made himself part of our little discussion group. "A mistake? There was no mistake," he said harshly. "She took up with some Italian gigolo, and left me crushed."

I saw Cat's confusion, and said to her with a wink, "Cat, this is my friend Ernest Hemingway."

"I'm sorry to be so brusque," Hemingway said. He put out his hand. "Nice to meet you, Cat. Now tell me about this mistake."

"I've heard the story many times but the man's name was always omitted. My great grandmother had one love in her life. She was set to follow him to America when catastrophe struck and she had to delay the trip. By the time she was able to travel, her lover had married someone else."

Slowly, as if his life depended on the answer, he said, "What catastrophe?"

"She was pregnant."

How does a room suddenly go silent yet there is sound all around? It seemed like a very long moment before anyone spoke, and it was Hemingway who broke the stillness. "That's not a reason to cancel her trip."

"She developed terrible morning sickness and couldn't travel."

"But why write and say she was engaged to someone else."

"She was afraid if she told you she was pregnant, you would feel obligated to marry her, even if you had changed your mind. She wanted to free you from any sense of commitment. "

"I loved her. Nothing would have changed that."

"Also she was worried about what your family might think of this unmarried, pregnant girl throwing herself at you."

Hemingway waved the comment aside. "I could give a crap what they thought." He paused. "Why didn't she come after the baby was born?"

"The baby was premature, and couldn't travel for more than a year. Apparently by that time you were engaged or married. I'm not sure which."

"The baby was a boy or girl?" I asked.

"A girl," Cat said.

Hemingway stared down at the floor for several seconds and then looked up at Cat. "Did Agnes ever marry?" he asked.

"No. My grandmother told me that Grandma Agnes felt she had found the one great love of her life, and there couldn't possibly be another. Besides, she had Catherine."

"That was the baby's name?" Hemingway asked.

"Yes, and Catherine became my grandmother. It's who I am named after - Catherine Agnes Telles, shortened to Cat."

We both watched Hemingway trying to digest these incredible revelations. I saw a myriad of emotions flitter across his face, while his eyes stared unseeing.

"Hem, are you okay?" I finally said.

He slowly shook his head. "All these years, I lived with anger, frustration, hurt, and even hate against a woman who truly loved me. How could I have been so blind as to take her letter at face value and not go back after her?" He looked at Cat. "If I had thought for a moment that letter was a lie, I would have swum the Atlantic Ocean to get to her."

I patted him gently on the shoulder. "I'm sorry we had to bring you this bad news."

Hemingway straightened up, and a smile slowly lit his face. "Bad news? Is it bad news that the person I have loved my whole life but thought I'd lost, has felt the same way towards me?" He gave a fist pump. "You can't believe the weight that has dropped off my heart. I almost feel alive again… if that were possible." His happiness radiated off of him like a heat lamp. Turning to Cat, he said, "Allow me to re-introduce my-self. I am Ernest Hemingway, your great grandfather."

Cat appeared moved but also a bit uncomfortable with the conversation. I leaned down. "Just go with the flow."

Hemingway wrapped an arm around each of us and pulled us to the bar. "Jake, I'll take another scotch and soda, while I need two empty glasses for my friends."

Jake slid two whisky tumblers in front of us, and moved to make Hemingway's drink. Pulling the flask that never seemed to empty from his hip pocket, he filled our glasses with his special whiskey.

I turned to Cat. "Better tell Jason he's going to be the lead singer for the rest of the night."

Cat laughed, took a deep sip, and went off toward the stage.

Hemingway lifted his new drink and we toasted. "I know why I am here now, Charley."

"I'm all ears."

"It was to heal a wound that so festered my heart that even after I was dead I couldn't rest comfortably. And at the same time a chance to meet my great, great granddaughter." We clicked glasses and drank. This Hemingway Whiskey was marvelous stuff.

He set his glass down, and then slowly turned 360 degrees taking in the whole scene. "I will miss this place." He turned back to me. "So did you get a few new chapters for that book you are writing?"

"Oh, I got more than a few." I lifted my glass to him. "Thanks for pushing me into the stream of humanity. I love it here, and don't plan on ever becoming a shoreline spectator again."

Cat was back, and now we started drinking and toasting seriously. The rest of the night was a blur, but I do remember at one point leaning into Hemingway's ear and saying, "I think I am in love with your granddaughter," or maybe I said that in Cat's ear. Whatever, it was the best dream I'd ever had.

When I awoke, the sun was beaming in through the windows. With eyes half shut, I glanced around and realized I was still in the Hemingway Heritage House, stretched out on his bed. As I surveyed the room, I saw that everything was the same as when I had fallen asleep. There was no makeshift table at the bedside. No bottle or empty glasses. No hangover. I glanced back in the hall and saw all my painting equipment spread out along the wall.

Laying back on the pillow, I felt a touch of sadness. It had all been a dream yet it had felt so real. And then I realized the positive side of the dream. I'd mentally gotten rid of my emotional baggage called Daphne. I was clearly over her. And I knew I was never going back to my constricted, controlled, boring life of old. In fact, I had even learned a few new dance moves which I couldn't wait to try again.

I smiled thinking of Cat. Was there even a band named Cat Black and the Midnight Howlers? What a name. Well, tonight I was calling in sick, and going down to Sloppy's and see who was singing there, and I was going to dance the socks off of somebody.

Yeah, what a dream. I closed my eyes and tried to bring up some of the good parts of the dream, but as most dreams do when we wake up, they had already begin to fade. I think I had started to doze off again, when a voice startled me.

"Hey, wild man, we have to get out of here before they start letting in the public."

I sat up. It was Cat just emerging from the bathroom, combing her hair.

"I moved the table back, and took care of the bottle and two glasses, but I'm not putting your painting crap away so get your butt up."

At least that's what I remember her saying. Cat claims it was a much more lady like comment, and I won't argue. Married couples argue enough as it is. One thing we didn't argue about was the name of our first son. And already, little Ernest is a handful. Probably gets it from his great, great grandfather.

*   *   *   *   *

Author's Note: This was a lot of fun to write. Hemingway has always fascinated me, and when I heard the title of a recent Kenny Chesney album - "Hemingway's Whiskey - I knew I had to write a story with that title. It helped that I was going down to the Florida Keys for a week. So in order to gain background, I spent a long enjoyable day in Key West at Hemingway's Heritage House, and Sloppy Joe's Bar. While at Sloppy Joe's, the Hemingway Look-A-Like Contest was just warming up. This goes on every year, and the winners become judges for the future competitions. It was quite a sight to see ten to fifteen Hemingways lined up at the bar, drinks in hand, smiling and laughing.

Cat Black was modeled after the lead singer who was there the night I enjoyed Sloppy's hospitality.

Agnes von Kurowsky existed and everything said about her was factual except the part about the pregnancy. She actually did leave Hemingway for an Italian army officer. Her loss and our gain, I rationalize, since some historians feel her desertion had a strong motivating effect on Hemingway's writing.

And last of all, who wouldn't like to dance like Fred Astaire and have a whole bar cheering them on.

Cupid's Arrow

The poets wax eloquent about it. The song writers immortalize it. The movies idolize it. But if you want the low-down-dirty on love, ask the guys you drink with. At least that's what they claim.

My house of philosophy is a small bar on the Upper West Side of New York called Nick and Al's. Every other Thursday we meet and solve not only our own, but also the world's problems - all in three hours, assisted of course by various fermented spirits.

Who needs a psychiatrist when you can present your thorny problems to such a laureate group - a car salesman, a New York's finest detective, an eminent judge, and a corporate accountant - and get an immediate answer, which of course, will change throughout the night.

It was on one of those insightful evenings that we stumbled into the question of whether love at first sight was possible. In other words, could two people see each other for the first time and just know it would be right. The analysis ran true to form, or should I say, true to occupation.

"It's like purchasing a new car without driving it," stated Ralph Ford, who paradoxically owned a Chevrolet dealership. "May look great on the outside, but once you take it for a spin, the seat doesn't feel right, the steering wheel is too stiff, and there's no pick up. No, you always want to test drive before you sign on the dotted line."

"So what you are saying," Eddie Giamona our Italian cop replied, "is that when you see some great babe that makes your heart race, you ask her if you can look under her hood before you become committed?"

"Only if she's got a great set of carburetors," Ralph replied, setting us all laughing.

"Gentlemen, gentlemen!" ventured our prominent judge, Jack Mentor, as he set his martini down. "You are reducing a very ethereal question to its basest level. I think that almost all romantic involvements are to some extent love at first sight. Maybe for some that so called 'first sight' occurs over an extended period. For example, take an office worker who sees a co-worker week after week with never a thought of romance, and then one day neither can exist without the other. Of course there are exceptions, but the most common reason for two people to go out is purely visual attraction, nothing deeper. There is no sudden lightning bolt of love that shoots out of the sky and throws them together."

He waved his empty glass at Lucy the bartender. "Take my job. Almost always on first perusal of the facts, I have an idea who's lying and who's not. But I never let first appearances determine my decision, even after all my years on the bench."

Dennis Farwood, a magician with numbers, raised his glass. "Nicely put, Jack, but I must disagree. What I love about numbers is that they never lie, but how you interpret them can be misleading." He paused. "Love at first sight? Clearly the physical appearance doesn't lie. What can be erroneous is your interpretation of the emotions that this physical attraction raises."

"You should have been a lawyer," Eddie the cop said. "You can complicate the simplest statements. Why don't you just tell it straight?"

"Which is?" Dennis replied, knowing Eddie's penchant for bottom line comments.

"What you see ain't necessarily what you get."

"Amen, brother," Ralph chimed in. He glanced around. "So we basically have four guys here who do not believe in love at first sight. Am I right?" He looked over at me. "And where do you sit on this, Mike?"

Mike Street, that's me. Perpetual bachelor at age thirty-six. No commitments, no responsibilities (unless you count one large dog), and no entanglements. In other words, no girlfriend. Just a number of dating companions.

I'd never been a believer in love at first sight, not in the slightest… until two weeks ago. Our paths had crossed in the lobby of my apartment building, as she was getting off the elevator and I was getting on. Long brown hair with the slightest tint of blond, flawless skin covering an attractive angular face, and a model's figure with its assertive strut.

As we passed, she looked straight into my eyes, held my gaze for just a moment longer than curiosity demanded, and then she was past me. Weak-kneed, heart pounding, I stood in the elevator and watched her stroll away. Just as the elevator doors were closing, she glanced back and winked.

I was two flights up before reason and sanity took over. Leaping to the control panel, I pushed the down button. Nothing. Just in time, I jabbed the third floor button. As the doors slide open, I raced to the stairwell. In seconds, I was on the street. She was nowhere in sight.

I approached the doorman sitting at his desk in the lobby. He was short and round with a rosy complexion, white hair, and wire rim glasses.

"Where is Mac, our usual doorman?" I asked.

"He's taking some time off. I'll be covering for him. Can I help you, sir?"

Up close, he appeared older than old, yet his eyes glowed with energy. I stuck out my hand. "I'm Mike Street, one of the tenants."

"And I'm Thornton," he said shaking my hand with a broad smile. "How can I help you, Mr. Street?"

"A woman just got off the elevator. She was tall, brown-haired, dressed in a black coat. Did you happen to see her?"

"It is my job to see everyone, sir. Yes, I noticed the young lady." He paused for a long moment and again smiled. "Is there anything else I can do for you sir?"

I grinned at him. "Thornton, you know what else you can do for me."

Tilting his head and still smiling, he said, "I am not a mind reader, Mr. Street."

"Who is she?" I asked. "The woman who came off the elevator."

"I have no idea, sir. This is my first night on duty." He arranged several items on his desk and then glanced up, "I am afraid it wouldn't matter if I did know. The rules state I cannot talk about the other tenants."

"Look, Thornton. Can't we work something out here? I really would like to meet this woman, and I think she wants to meet me."

"How wonderful for you, sir. Although, we can only guess at the lady's response to your entreaties," he said.

I laughed. "You got me there." After a moment, I said, "All I'm asking is that you let me know the next time she comes in. Just call my apartment, and I'll come right down."

I cut off any potential negative response. "You don't have to do anything except call me. That's fair isn't it?"

He rearranged the same items on his desk, and then looked up. "Very reasonable, Mr. Street."

It had now been two weeks with no call from Thornton. My guess was that she was more likely a visitor than a tenant. My hope was she might be visiting again.

"Hey, Mike! You here with us tonight?" Ralph yelled. "What's your opinion on this love at first sight?"

"Not sure," I replied, deciding to leave my recent experience out of the discussion. "What do you think, Lucy?" I asked, deflecting attention away from me.

Lucy was the epitome of what every man wants his bartender to look like. Tall, blond, attractive, and shapely. We all had a crush on her, but since she was happily married, she'd evolved into the group's big sister. Year after year, she had endured our alcoholic discussions and now probably knew us as well as our families and friends.

"You, gentlemen, have it all wrong. It has nothing to do with love at first sight. Love is about fate. It's the gods' decree that decides it."

"You been hitting the sauce tonight?" Eddie said with a smirk.

"Give me trouble, copper, and I'll cuff you to a bathroom stall," she snarled, adding a smile.

Eddie raised his hands in surrender. "Hey, I never spoke."

When Lucy got going on a subject, it was always entertaining. As a professional student with ten years of classes at Columbia, she could add new dimensions to any discussion.

"I am a believer of fate," she continued. "When Cupid unleashes his golden arrow, it doesn't matter if it is the first time you've seen someone, or you've known them for years, your fate is sealed."

"Puhleeze....Don't give us a lot of crap about some winged fat boy with an archery set," Eddie pleaded.

Lucy flicked her towel at him. "Cupid is from Greek mythology. His father is Mars, the God of war, and his mother is Venus, the God of human love. When Venus decides that two people should be in love that is what we call fate. It's Cupid's job to assist in the attainment of her wishes."

"And the feathered missiles?" Jack asked, and then pointed to his martini. "By the way, this is one of your better creations."

"Thanks, Judge. As for the arrows, those are merely symbols of his active role rather than a literal interpretation. Actually, he'll use any means at his disposal to fulfill his mother's desire that two people should meet and fall in love."

"We apparently have an authority on love and mythology in our midst," Jack said, raising his now empty glass in a silent toast.

Lucy nodded back at him and glanced around. "Refills anyone?"

When she returned with our orders, I asked her, "Getting back to this question of love at first sight, what if you see this person only once and then never again?"

Lucy paused in setting down a drink, her lips pursed in thought. "Then I guess it wasn't meant to be."

Grasping for some thread of encouragement for my own predicament, I asked, "What is this about Cupid using any means to help the situation?"

Lucy leaned up against the liquor cabinet behind her. "According to mythology, Cupid is invisible. There is, though, some vague legend, source unknown, that Cupid can assume an earthly shape to help bring two people together." She scrunched her face up in thought. "I seem to remember that as part of that legend he will reappear once more in that same form when the two have been brought together."

"Any more of this and I want waders," Eddie cried. "The bullshit level is at an all-time high."

Ralph stood and bowed toward Lucy. "I'm convinced. You could sell cars on my lot anytime, Lucy."

Lucy leaned into Eddie's face. "You want all time high bullshit? Sometime, stop and listen to your pick up lines."

As we all laughed, Lucy wet the tip of her index finger and marked a one in the air.

Eddie pointed at her, "Italians never forget."

Lucy grinned sweetly. "Can I have high heels for my cement shoes?"

After a few more rounds of companionable insults, the night ended. In the taxi home, I mulled over Lucy's comments and decided that my situation was a one-view episode destined for nothing.

I had just fallen asleep when the phone rang. Fumbling for the receiver, I mumbled, "Yeah?"

"Mr. Street? This is Thornton. I would suggest you come straight away to the lobby."

Now I was wide awake. "Is she there?"

"I will merely say that there is a person of interest who is just leaving."

I leaped out of bed. "Keep her there. Ask her some questions. Find out who she is. Anything. I will be right down!"

Dressing was a blur of action, thoughts, and hopes. Racing down the stairs, I realized I had forgotten shoes. I burst into the lobby and it was empty, except for Thornton at his desk.

"Where did she go?" I pleaded. He nodded toward the front entrance. "You can catch her if you hurry, sir."

I charged through the door. She was halfway down the block

getting into a taxi.

"Wait!" I yelled.

She seemed to hesitate but then continued to climb into the cab.

"Stop," I cried, starting to run. I had taken only a few long strides when my foot hit a puddle. It was like hitting the proverbial banana peel. My feet flew up, I was airborne, and then everything went black.

"Mr. Street. Mr. Street," the voice said gently.

Very slowly I eased open my eyes. The sky was white. No, it wasn't sky, it was a ceiling. And instead of the hard sidewalk, I was in a soft bed. The equipment around me, the buzzing and clamor of people racing about, the overhead paging, told me I was in a hospital.

"Hello, Mr. Street. I'm Dr. Whitmore. You are in the emergency room at St. Mary's Hospital. Do you remember what happened?"

"Vaguely," I slowly replied. "I was running, I slid on something, and then wham!!" I glanced around. "How did I get here?"

"You took a bad fall, struck the back of your head, and were knocked unconscious. Your doorman saw it all and called 911. You arrived here just a few minutes ago."

"Oh, man I cannot believe this," I said shaking my head, which was definitely the wrong maneuver. The shooting pain in the back of my skull felt like someone had just driven a railroad spike into it. I grabbed it in agony, only to find my fingers buried in a large fluffy bandage.

The doctor saw my grimacing. "I'm afraid your head is going to be pretty sore for a while. We put a bandage on to stop the bleeding. Once I finish my neuro exam and get a CT of your head, I'll stitch up your scalp laceration. Somewhere along the way, our on-call neurosurgeon will come by and exam you."

"Do I really need all this? Can't you just sew me up and I'm out of here?"

"You received quite a blow to your head, enough so that you were unconscious for almost ten minutes. You definitely need the CT and, as for the neurosurgeon, Dr. Johnson is already here seeing another patient. You are going to need follow up when you get released, and that will be with Dr. Johnson."

"Yeah, okay." I lay back down on the bed and closed my eyes. I felt drained as the adrenaline from my injury wore off and the post-traumatic let down set in. It didn't help that I had been drinking before all of this. Despite the noise and my headache, I must have fallen asleep. In my dreams I vaguely felt something on my shoulder. I pulled away and slipped back into dreamland.

"Mr. Street!" This time something had a real grip on my shoulder and was shaking it.

When I opened my eyes and finally got the room in focus, I realized that my head injury was more serious then I had been lead to believe. Hallucinations could not be a good sign after head trauma, and I was definitely hallucinating.

Standing next to me, like an angel from on high, was my "love at first sight."

I blinked several times trying to clear my vision. The hallucination remained.

"Hi, I'm Dr. Johnson the neurosurgeon. The ER physician wanted me to check you over."

"Oh, there is a God," I whispered softly.

"I'm sorry, what did you say?" she asked.

"Please go ahead and let me check you over."

She looked at me like I had grown another head.

"I mean… check me over."

As she performed her examination, I tried not to stare and hoped I wasn't drooling. Up close, her nose was a bit crooked and teeth a little uneven, but it just added to her beauty, making her more real and not so untouchable. Even her voice was a pleasure to hear.

Finished, she placed her examination tools into a black bag and turned to me. "You have had a concussion which means you were knocked out. There is nothing to suggest anything more serious, such as a brain contusion, which is actual damage to the brain. To be safe, though, let's get a CT of your head and watch you overnight. We should be able to send you home in the morning. Any questions?"

Oh, yes, there were questions but not about my head injury. "You look familiar," I said. "I think we might be neighbors."

She arched her eyebrows.

"Don't you live in the Gramercy Apartment Building?"

She smiled and shook her head. "I don't, but my brother has an apartment there."

"Ah," I replied, still easing into it. "I think we ran into each other coming out of the elevator a while back."

She stared at me with her beautiful eyes and then shrugged her shoulders. "I'm sure that's possible, but I'm terrible at remembering faces." She gently shifted the subject back to my health. "Now in regards to your hospital stay."

I wasn't going to let her off so easily. It was time to quit easing and start jumping into it.

"This may seem a bit forward…" I was cut off as a nurse leaned into the room and said, "Dr. Johnson. Phone for you. It's your husband."

"Thank you," she replied and turned back to me. "You were

saying?"

I was saying nothing. My entire cerebral function had seized up and gone into lock down.

"Mr. Street?"

I finally croaked out, "Just wanted to thank you."

"You are welcome. I'll see you in the morning."

And with that she was out the door, and any belief I had in love at first sight was gone with her.

Early in the morning, Dr. Johnson whisked in, assured me I was fine, gave me a golden smile, and then rushed out. Definitely no connection between us other than patient and doctor. I thought about the stare and the wink that day at the elevator. Maybe I'd caught her in an unguarded moment. Maybe I'd imagined the wink. Maybe I needed to get a life and move on.

"Mr. Street. What happened to you?" It was Mac, our regular doorman and he was back at his post. I probably looked as bad as I felt as I shuffled across the apartment building lobby.

"Long story, Mac. Say, where's Thornton?"

"He's off to a new job. This just wasn't his cup of tea. Going to be working for his mother, if you can believe that."

Two days later I was walking home from work and just about to enter my apartment building when a taxicab pulled up. The door opened and my heart missed a beat. Climbing out was Dr. Johnson. While trying to balance several packages, she fumbled around in her purse for the fare.

"Here, let me," I said pulling out my wallet. "It's the least I can do for what you did for me."

"And what did I do for you?" she asked, smiling.

"The hospital, the care, etc."

"Oh, that." Her smile broadened. After a moment's hesitation, she said, "Didn't we run into each other at the elevator a few weeks ago?"

Now she remembers. And don't you have a husband I wanted to say.

I could see the fare on the meter. It was eight dollars so I handed the cabbie a twenty. He looked up at me, smiled, and drove off. I was so shocked by what I'd seen that I barely heard what she said behind me.

"Can you help me with these packages while I find my key?"

Totally distracted, I grabbed the parcels and we went into the lobby. She produced her apartment key, and took the packages from me. Giving me a questioning look, she walked into the open elevator.

I was still thinking about the cabbie when she reached out and stopped the elevator door from closing.

"Oh, by the way, Dr. Johnson is my twin sister," she said, "but feel free to thank me for whatever she did." And just as the door closed she winked at me.

It was a moment before her words sank in, and another moment to savor the wink. I was all grins and standing on a cloud, when I turned toward Mac.

"You told me that Thornton had quit and gone to work for his mother. What line of work is she in?"

He chuckled. "She runs some kind of dating service. V's Match-ups, or something like that. Not sure how he'll fit into it."

I thought back to the cabbie as he took my twenty dollars. The smile he flashed had not been about the money. No, Thornton in his role as a cabbie, had been smiling about something else. I didn't remember seeing anything on the front seat of the cab next to him, but I guess with changing times you modernize your methods. Bows and arrows have become passé.

*   *   *   *   *

Author's Notes: Is there such a thing as love at first sight? I think there is, for I still remember exactly where and when I first saw my wife. And was it love at first sight? I'm not sure, but seeing her definitely changed the course of my life.

This story was inspired by an O'Henry short story - "Mammon and the Archer" - a beautiful tale if you have never read it. In the short story, Cupid is described as a fat boy without clothes shooting arrows around with a bow, and felt to have no role in the romance that ensued. I took the opposite stand, and chose the concept that Cupid might appear in any shape, and actually have a hand in directing a romance. Thus was born the basis for this story.

The Thief of Hearts

One would think that a man who parachuted into inaccessible areas to fight forest fires - a smoke-jumper - who'd been mauled by a mountain lion, who'd dropped a charging, crazed grizzly with one perfect shot, wouldn't be afraid of anything.

Well, there was nothing that John Brand feared, except what now stood in front of him. Five foot seven with reddish brown hair and a trim athletic figure.

"I'll have a mocha grande, please," she said, a flash of white teeth accompanying her wide smile.

John turned to make the drink and glanced down at his hands. If they had shaken when he took aim at that bear like they were shaking now, he'd be on the wrong side of the grass in some lonely cemetery.

While he steamed the milk, he glanced over at her. Someday he'd speak to her, ask her out, and they'd...

"Damn," he cried, yanking his hand back from the scalding steam jet and dropping the metal milk pitcher onto the floor.

Unbelievable, he told himself. This was becoming a joke. Every time she came in, he dropped something, spilled something, made the wrong order, or whatever. He had become King Klutz around the shop.

He turned, not meeting her eyes. "Sorry. I'll be just a minute more."

"I'm in no rush." Her voice was so melodic that her words sounded like a song.

Get your act together, he thought. Concentrate!

John Brand had been about to start his two month vacation from the forestry service when his Uncle Bill called. He asked if John could help cover the shop for a few weeks while Bill took his wife down to L.A. for a complicated surgery. Since Bill had paid his way through college, John never hesitated in his reply.

So now he covered the morning shift at his uncle's espresso shop in Carmel. The work was fun, a real change of pace from his firefighting duties. In the two weeks he'd been there, he'd fallen in love with the quaint, seaside town. Unfortunately, he had fallen for more than just Carmel.

Could you be in love with someone you'd never spoken to except to take her coffee order every morning for two weeks? It was a question he asked himself every day just before she came in for her espresso. Always for a mocha grande. Always with a beautiful golden retriever that she tied up outside the door in the small patio.

He poured the single shot of espresso into the steamed chocolate milk.

"Whipped cream?" he asked looking up at her. He already knew the answer, but he just wanted to watch her lips form the words.

"Just a dab," she replied with a warm smile.

Brand felt his heart do the usual flip flops when she spoke to him and wondered if he should see a doctor. He'd had fires nearly engulf him, once he'd had to bury himself in the ground while a fire burned over him, and yet never had he felt the slightest change in his heart rhythm. Maybe he was getting old. Probably he was just drinking too much espresso.

He watched her walk out onto the patio and disappear around the edge of the building. He knew she sat at the same corner table with her dog and read the paper every morning.

"Why don't you ask her out?"

Brand glanced over at Melissa, the girl he worked with each morning. Short, dyed-blond hair, nose ring, and four sets of ear rings. She grinned at him.

"Who?" John replied, trying to cover his embarrassment.

Melissa laughed. "One guess and it's not the dog."

"Oh, her. Yeah, seems like a nice person."

"Well, either you ask her out, and by the way her name is Liz, or I'm going to tell her to stop coming in."

John raised his eyebrows.

"At the rate you're going, if she keeps dropping in, you'll have this place destroyed in a couple more weeks."

They stared at each other for a moment, and then they both started laughing.

"Yeah," John said. "I've got it bad."

"So, speak to her."

"Not that simple."

"I don't see you having trouble talking with the other women that come in here."

"They don't look like her." He took a deep breath. "When I was a junior in high school, I fell head-over-heels for a senior. It took me six months to work up the courage to ask her out." He paused, a faraway look in his eyes.

"Yeah?"

"I wasn't always the suave and debonair guy I am now," he said with a grin.

"And she turned you down?"

"In spades. Dropped my confidence level with women through the soles of my shoes."

"Are you telling me you never asked a girl out since?

"I've done my share of dating."

"So what's the problem here? I'm lost."

"This girl looks almost exactly like my senior heart-throb."

Melissa cocked her head to one side. "And you're afraid this is going to be a re-run. High School Catastrophe Part II?"

"Something like that."

Melissa moved off to help several customers. It was an hour-and-a-half later before business slowed enough for them to talk.

"I've got a solution," Melissa offered.

Something in her voice caused John to look up from the coffee grinder he was filling. He caught a strange smile, just disappearing.

"I think I'll pass," he said.

"No! This is great!" she said, and then her excitement changed to concern. "Promise me you won't think I'm crazy."

Oh, this is going to be a beauty of an idea, John thought. "Melissa, I'll work this out. No reason for you to get involved."

"My grandmother was a full-blooded Sioux Indian. Lived on the reservation until she died. I used to spend long parts of my summer vacation with her."

"Interesting," John said, pouring the coffee beans.

"We'd spend hours talking, especially when I was in my teens. I was having boy problems. Things I couldn't speak to my mother about." She said smiling. "There was this one boy I really had a crush on, but he didn't even know I was on the same planet. I dreamed about him day and night.

"Finally, my grandmother told me that if I really wanted the boy, she had a way. It was a magic potion."

John stopped his pouring. "A magic potion? Don't tell me this is your plan to help me."

"No, listen. She told me if someone drank the potion, they would be totally captivated by the next person that spoke to them. The spell would last about two hours."

"Captivated, but not in love?"

"No, not in love. But grandmother said if a man was totally captivated by me and I couldn't win his heart in two hours, then he wasn't meant for me."

"What happened when you tried it?"

Melissa sighed. "By the time I got home that summer, his family had moved away." She shrugged her shoulders. "Never found anyone else I wanted to try it on. Besides, there is only enough for one dose."

He looked at her askance. "And you were offering to let me use it?"

Melissa grinned. "Don't get all mushy on me, John."

"What's this potion called?"

"The Thief of Hearts. Great name, huh?"

John nodded. "Thanks, but it's not for me. I don't want to win her with magic potions."

"It doesn't 'win her;' it just makes her focus on you for about two hours. You still have to do all the winning. This just gives you a chance."

John smiled and shook his head.

Melissa shrugged. "Whatever you say, John. But this is a once in a lifetime opportunity."

When John opened the shop the next morning, he vowed this would be the day. He'd introduce himself, make some small talk, and then ask her out. What the hell. High school was a long time ago.

"Morning, John," Melissa said, bursting through the front door. "Ready for the big day?"

John raised his eyebrows. "What big day?"

"You're going to ask her out today, aren't you?"

"What are you, clairvoyant?"

An hour later Liz strolled into the shop. Melissa gave John an elbow in the side as he moved to the counter.

"Hi," he said. "The usual?"

She smiled at him. "I'm surprised you remember, with so many customers each day."

This was it. The opening he wanted. He leaned forward to speak and the phone rang. He glanced around, waiting for Melissa to appear and answer it, but no such luck.

After four rings, he said "Excuse me" and walked over and picked up the phone. The caller was his Uncle Bill.

"You had me worried for a moment when no one answered the phone. Thought my business might have gone down the toilet."

Melissa appeared from around the corner. John covered the receiver with his hand. "Can you make a mocha grande? I'm going to be tied up for a few minutes. It's Uncle Bill."

Melissa saw who it was at the counter and a strange look crossed her face.

Uh, oh, John thought, but then Bill's voice pulled him back to the call. Bill went on at length about his wife's successful surgery and her uneventful post-operative course. Everything was going great. And how was the business doing?

By the time John could free himself, his heart-throb had taken her mocha and gone outside. He shook his head at another missed opportunity.

"Go talk to her. Now!" Melissa said.

The urgency in her voice surprised him and then he grasped the sound of her voice "You didn't!" he exclaimed, his eyes widening.

"Yes, I put the potion in her mocha. The next person to speak to her will captivate her, entrance her, whatever, for the next two hours." She pushed him toward the door. "So get your butt out there before she speaks to someone else!"

What the heck, he decided, pulling off his apron. Now or never. He tucked in his shirt and stepped on to the patio.

There she sat at a corner table, the morning paper spread in front of her, and, thank God, no one was speaking to her. John paused in mid-stride and started wondering. Why am I worried if someone is speaking to her? Do I really have any faith in this magic brew? What did she call it? The Thief of Hearts? Well, if nothing else, it's stolen my ability to think if I believe in such a thing. He resumed his course to her table.

"Hi," he said, his heart hammering against his chest. "Mind if I join you for a few minutes?"

He tried to read the thoughts buried in the deep greenish-brown eyes that glanced up at him. He looked for captivation, entrancement, longing, interest. Instead, he should have been looking for her dog.

Out of nowhere, the dog leaped up on him, knocking him to the ground. As the dog stood on him, saliva dripping from its growling, snarling jaws, John found himself shocked at the size a golden retriever could achieve and more so at the length of their teeth.

"Good doggie," he managed to croak out. In that instant, something in the dog's dark menacing eyes changed and he brought his mouth down on John's neck.

I'm dead, he thought, as he struggled to get his hands up and push the huge beast away. He felt wetness on his neck. Is that blood? And then his fear changed to surprise. The wetness was saliva. This gigantic, furry killer was licking his neck and now his face, whining and barking. John managed to roll out from under the dog, pushing him away as he continually tried to lick him, all the while leaping and barking.

"Oh, I'm so sorry," the girl said, moving quickly to the dog. She could barely pull it away, for the dog kept trying to lick John's hands and rub up against his legs.

His entrance and dignity shattered, John brushed himself off and sat down at the table. Almost immediately, the dog pulled away from Liz, ran over and laid his head in John's lap.

Well, this is better than his jaws at my throat, John thought as he stroked the animal's head, rubbing him behind the ears. The dog responded with a low, throaty growl, almost a purr.

"What's his name?" John asked, staring over at Liz who now sat across from him, her mouth agape.

"Leo," she stammered her own eyes like saucers.

"Nice dog. Although, I think he needs to work on his introduction."

The woman just nodded, staring at John with a dumbfounded look.

Man, she really is captivated, John thought. This is great, but I'd hoped there might be more give and take in our conversation.

"I don't think we've ever been introduced," he said." My name's John Brand. I'm filling in here for a few weeks to help the owner, who's my uncle."

Once again, the girl just nodded. No verbal response followed.

This potion is definitely too strong, John concluded. Glancing around, he spotted her empty mocha glass. That's it. She drank it too fast and the effects were maximized. Maybe you're just supposed to sip it.

He nodded toward her empty glass. "How was the mocha?"

The woman's attention shifted slowly from him to the glass. It was a moment before she spoke. "The mocha's not for me," she replied. "It's for Leo. He loves them."

John spied a small dog dish on the ground under the table, remnants of the mocha still visible on the bottom.

Liz continued. "Gives me time to read the newspaper."

John looked down at the dog staring up at him. His eyes radiated captivation, entrancement, and fascination.

He put back his head and started laughing.

"What's so funny?" Liz asked.

"Life," he said, standing up. "Thanks for letting me join you." The dog began to rub its head back and forth against John's leg. "Do you have a leash for Leo?"

As if in a daze, the girl pulled one from her purse. John snapped it on Leo then tied the other end to the table.

"I've got to get back to work. Have a nice day," he said and walked back toward the shop's entrance. Behind him he could hear Leo barking and howling while his mistress tried to quiet him down.

When he reached the counter, Melissa immediately walked over.

"So?"

"The dog drank it. Enough said."

"The dog?" She leaned back against the counter, thought about it for a moment, and then roared with laughter. "That is just too good. Ten years of hoarding that potion. Waiting for the right man to come along, only to have it given to a dog." She stopped laughing, suddenly serious. "Did you get a date... with the dog?" She roared again with laughter.

"Not remotely funny," John said. "And I don't want to hear another word about her or her dog. I'm over them both." He shook his head with disgust. "You and your magic potion. What the hell was I thinking?"

Business picked up and was fast and furious for a half an hour before slowing. John was cleaning glasses when Melissa tapped him on the shoulder.

"Someone wants to speak to you," she said.

John glanced over at the counter and saw Liz staring at him. He dried his hands and walked over. Now what? he thought.

She smiled at him, clearly a bit nervous. "I'm not very good at this, but I was wondering, if you're free some night, would you like to go out with me?"

John's mouth dropped and it was his turn to be the silent conversationalist.

"I know this is a surprise. Please don't think I make a habit of asking strange men out."

John tried to speak but couldn't.

She rushed on. "Leo has been my companion and protector for years. Never before has he shown anything but aggression toward any man who came near me." She glanced back over her shoulder. "Out on the patio, his behavior was so unusual, it left me speechless." She took in a breath and slowly let it out. "So I decided that whatever it was that Leo saw in you, I wanted a chance to see it myself."

* * * * *

Author's Note: There was a time when I would spend several hours a week at a local coffee shop. The characters in this story were loosely modeled after the baristas in that store.

Somewhere along the line, I picked up the phrase, "The Thief of Hearts," and it became the title for this tale even before the story idea was conceived. Several times in the past I have developed titles, and then written narratives that fulfill these titles (e.g., Hemingway's Whiskey) Not always the easiest way to approach creating a story, but it does make an exciting journey.

Airport Poker

We were three bored men killing time in a deserted airport, waiting for a delayed flight. Three strangers staring into our beers, our thoughts a million frequent flyer miles away. Occasionally, one of us would make a comment about the USC-UCLA football game on the wide screen TV.

Neal, the guy to my right, had gone to USC and let us know it whenever they scored.

I was a UCLA alumnus, but never developed the rah-rah spirit so suffered through it in silence.

On the far side of Neal was Fred who'd boisterously introduced himself when he joined our intimate group of two about thirty minutes before. He seemed neutral about the outcome.

Conversation had been minimal and primarily football related. We'd just witnessed another USC touchdown, when Fred blurted out, "Hey, I got an idea," he said. "A little game. Winner's bar tab is covered by the losers. How about it?"

While the bartender brought us another round, Fred enthusiastically explained the game to Neal and me.

"You place some object on the bar, some treasure that you carry with you, and tell a story connected to it. The guy with the best story wins."

"What the hell kind of game is that?" Neal asked, shaking his head. "Think I carry trophies around in my pocket? Lists of my life's accomplishments?"

"No," Fred replied. "You're missing the point. It could be anything. Your watch, a special tie, a pen. Anything. What's important is the story attached to it." He looked at the two of us. "So, you guys in or out?"

"Ah, what the hell," Neal said. "Nothing else to do."

"Why don't you start then," Fred said.

Neal thought a moment and then began. "It was 1968 and I was in New York City interviewing for a job. I'd stepped into an elevator behind a crowd of other people. Since I was closest to the elevator buttons, several people asked me to press their floor numbers. Lastly, someone in the back requested floor 26. I reached up and pressed the button with the finger my school ring was on." He held up his hand and flashed us his USC class ring. "Gradually the elevator emptied, until it was just myself and the guy who had asked for floor 26.

"As the elevator approached his floor, he moved up and stood next to me. 'From your ring, I see that you're a USC graduate,' he ventured. I turned to look at him and recognition was instant. I reached out my hand, and said, 'Good luck tomorrow.' He smiled, we shook, and then he stepped out of the elevator.

Once again, Neal lifted his hand and displayed his ring. "The man on the elevator with me was O. J. Simpson, and the next day he was awarded the Heisman trophy."

He glanced back and forth at the two of us. "So how is that for a story?"

"Pretty good," I said.

"Yeah, not bad," Fred added.

"So who's next?" Neal asked.

"How about if I go second?" Fred said.

"Fine with me," I replied.

Fred took a pull from his beer and then got a confident cat

smile. Slipping his wrist watch off, he dropped it on the bar. It was a Rolex, and even from two barstools away I could tell it was the real thing.

"I was in Desert Storm, a first lieutenant in an infantry division called up from the reserves. Never had shot at anyone, much less been to war. We'd been there only a few days when we saw our first action. Let me tell you, I was scared. I didn't want to die. Didn't want to come home without a piece of my body. Hell, I had a family and two kids."

Neal nodded. "Know exactly how you felt. I spent a month in Bosnia on UN patrol."

"So we're following this armored tank group that is moving fast," Fred continued. "Suddenly we're getting shelled and rockets are exploding all around us. I start looking for cover and realize that I'm out in the middle of the frigging desert and the only cover is sand." He takes a sip of beer. "The guy next to me disappears into bits and pieces of red meat. 'Shit, I've got to move,' I tell myself. I sprint to a tank that's halted in front of me and dive under the back end. Shells going off all around and I'm curled into a ball under this huge metal giant, remembering prayers I hadn't thought of since kindergarten.

"Just when I think it's all over, that I'm going to make it, a rocket hits my tank." Fred's hands flew up and apart. "Boom! The explosion was so strong; it blew me out from under the tank. I was lying there dazed, trying to remember what happened. After a bit, a corpsman knelt down beside me, did a quick exam, and told me to lie still for a while. Someone would be by for me."

Fred lifts the watch and stares at it. "So I'm lying there, thanking God for His mercy, when I hear a voice. Actually, just the barest whisper of a voice. I look around and no one is near me. I hear it again and realized that it was coming from inside the damaged tank."

He looks to make sure we're tuned in. "There is someone inside calling for help." He pauses dramatically. "Mind you, there's no one else around, the tank is on fire, and I've used up all my luck for the day."

Another sip of beer.

"But the guy keeps calling; only now his voice is even weaker. Finally I thought, what the hell. I check to see that everything is working, and then staggered over to the one area of the tank that's not in flames. Somehow I climb up and crawl to the open hatch. The heat from the flames is horrendous. I'm about to jump back off when I see this guy inside looking up at me. He's injured and too weak to get out on his own. I reach down, grab him by the shirt, and wrestle him out of the tank. I don't know where I got the strength, but next thing I know we're both lying on the sand and the tank is nothing but a burned cinder.

Fred held up the watch. "The guy I pulled out sent this to me a year later." He looked around. "So do you want to just pay my tab now?"

Neal banged his beer mug down. "How could anyone top that?" Then he glared at Fred, understanding dawning in his eyes. "And how many other dumb schmucks like us have you pulled in with this game of yours?"

Fred smiled. "Let's just say I haven't paid a bar tab for a long time." He started to rise, but I grabbed his wrist.

"Game's not over yet," I said quietly.

He sat back down, a cynical smile playing on his lips. "You got something better?"

I tossed an object onto the bar. It rolled dizzily around then settled on its back.

"You're going to match my Rolex, my story, with an old button?" Fred said.

Neal leaned forward. "Let's hear his story, Fred. You worried you might finally have to pay a bar tab?"

Fred laughed. "No chance, so let's hear it."

I took a long drink from my beer and began. "It was a number of years ago. I was in a relationship that was having real problems, but I was too obtuse to recognize them. I thought we had arrived at what all relationships mature into, yet even I could tell that something was lacking. About this time, I met a woman at work who shattered my one-to-ten scale."

"I like this story already," Neal chimed in.

"The first time we met, it was like a bear had suddenly grabbed me and squeezed all the air from my lungs. I could barely wheeze out, "Hello." Over the next few months I wondered if I was developing asthma, until I realized that the shortness of breath spells only occurred around her. Fortunately for my lungs, she got engaged, and with her now out of my potential dating pool, my physical response to her slipped back toward normal.

"Time passed and circumstances occasionally threw us together on work-related projects. On one such occasion, we had finished our work and were waiting for our boss to arrive. I began asking her questions about her background, more to be polite than anything else. Remember, I had initially been attracted to this woman because, well you know, her physical appearance, but with her responses, I discovered she was so much more. Adjectives like intelligent, humorous, compassionate were inadequate. She was like a fountain of life, a person who exuded some aura that enveloped me, made me want to grab life with all ten fingers, dive into it, and swim through it. And I wanted to do it all with her.

"We began to meet outside work. In the beginning it was just to talk about the office, but eventually we started to talk about our lives, our problems. She was having misgivings about her fiancé. She doubted his love for her, and even wondered if he wasn't seeing an old girlfriend on the side. I tried to give her an objective, unbiased opinion."

"I'll bet it was unbiased," Fred cut in.

"I tried to explain how men thought, why they acted the way they did. I even attempted to defend her fiancé, but my heart wasn't in it. He didn't seem like the man for her. Meanwhile, I had let slip some of my own problems in my relationship. I was finally beginning to realize that the major hurdle in my relationship was plain old lack of love. I really cared for my companion, but I wasn't in love with her. And I suspected she probably felt the same."

Fred pointed to his Rolex. "We have a plane coming soon. Is there going to be some excitement to this story, or just the usual boy meets girl?"

I ignored him. "I can't remember the exact circumstances, but somehow we made a date for lunch on a day we both had free.

"It was a typical Seattle spring day, wet and dreary, when I picked her up. We were soaked by the time we reached my car. Of course my radio was broken and the heater was stuck on high, yet sitting at the ferry terminal, everything seemed perfect. As we drove onto the ferry, I felt like I was in a movie. A love story where the two stars that everyone had been waiting to see get together were finally doing just that.

"I don't remember what we spoke about on the trip over to Bainbridge Island. The only thing of importance was that she was there with me, and I was going to have her for the whole afternoon.

"We went to a small Italian restaurant overlooking the water. The wait was so long she joked that that's how waiters got their names. I chuckled, and realized that we were both a bit uncomfortable. This was a date. In the past, it had always been a short run-in at work or a brief meeting for coffee. But this was definitely a date. Two people sitting in a romantic restaurant on the bay. One living with someone and the other engaged to be married. So not surprisingly, we felt very awkward. The right place at the wrong time.

"'Would you like something to drink?' our waiter asked. 'Two glasses of champagne,' I replied, hoping to loosen things up. We sat and sipped while making polite, noncommittal conversation. By the second round, though, we started to open up. I found myself looking into eyes that were so expressive, so sexy, so whatever I wanted them to be, that it scared me.

"Finishing the second glass, my companion excused herself and went to the bathroom. She was gone about five minutes and I began to worry. Then she reappeared, looking even more beautiful than when she had left, if that was possible. She sat down, and as we began to talk, I noticed that her shirt had become partially unbuttoned. In fact, two of the five buttons on the shirt were undone exposing some very distracting cleavage. For the first time, I found my thoughts moving from romance and flowers to wondering how I could get my hands on the other three buttons.

"I tried to avert my eyes since mouth-open-ogling is poor form. We held off on further champagne but since neither of us had eaten before the date, the damage was done. For the next hour-and-a-half, we laughed, we giggled, and we flirted. I never even tried to flee, but offered myself fully to the tsunami of her eyes, her smile, her personality, and, yes, her body. My eyes drifted toward that open shirt more times than I would like to admit."

My story was halted by the announcement that our delayed flight had finally arrived and would be boarding in ten minutes.

"You'd better finish this up," Neal said, downing the last of his beer.

"We left the restaurant and went out to my car. I opened the door to let her in. She turned to thank me and suddenly we were kissing. I don't know who started it but it just kept going.

Realizing I might need this kiss to last me a lifetime, passion, lust, and desire were left in the dust with the ferocity of our embrace.

"On the ferry ride back, we were surprised yet excited about this unexpected outcome. I sheepishly admitted that her blouse was partially undone and that I had meant to tell her but it slipped my mind. She laughed and gave her own confession. She had purposely unbuttoned her shirt in the bathroom wanting to look sexy. Her only excuse was the champagne.

"'I'd call that 'a two button lunch,' I told her. 'If you ever break off your engagement, I want to take you out for a five-button dinner.'

"'My blouse only has five buttons,' she answered.

"'I know,' I responded, sitting back having finished my story.

Neal and Fred were silent for a moment. It was Neal who spoke first. He pointed at the button on the bar. "So what's that all about?"

"That's the fifth button," I replied. I held up my left hand, the light flashing off my wedding ring. "And that's who lives with me now." I then pulled my sleeve back, exposing my wrist-watch. "And that's who bought this time piece for me," I said, staring at my companions.

Fred insisted on paying the whole tab.

Neal and Fred had drifted off to the plane and I was finishing my beer when the bartender approached. "I couldn't help but overhear your game," she said. "Don't get me wrong, but I thought the second gentleman's story was a little better. I'm surprised he paid up so quickly without an argument."

"I thought his story was better too." I looked up and smiled. "Too bad it wasn't true."

"How do you know that?"

"If they are firing rockets, trying to hit tanks, the last thing a tank will do is stop and become a sitting target. And the last place you want to hide is behind a target."

The bartender thought for a moment. "But he didn't know that you knew that. So why did he pay up?"

"He suspected I knew he was lying. You remember my comment about the watch my wife gave me. That comment was for him and he knew it. I would guess that's where he got his Rolex. After all, who would give you something like that except your wife?"

The bartender shook her head. "Boy, you can't trust anyone these days."

"You sure can't."

I stood to leave.

"What kind of work are you in?" she asked.

"Professional poker player."

She laughed. "So his hand was a Rolex and you beat it with a button."

I was walking away, when she called after me." Hey, you forgot your button."

I looked back and smiled. "Keep it. I found it on the floor." I stopped when I saw her crestfallen look and shook my head. "The reason I picked up that button," I told her, smiling at the button, "was it looked like my wife's fifth button."

* * * * *

Author's Note: On a trip to the Virgin Islands, I met a man who had sailed his catamaran all the way around from Los Angeles. Not an easy journey since he had a prosthetic leg. He'd been involved in World War II as a tank driver. His vehicle had been hit by a shell, leaving it extensively damaged and on fire. Everyone else in the tank was dead, and he couldn't move because of his leg injury. He kept calling for help and was about to give up, when he heard a voice outside. His rescuer reached down inside, pulled him from the tank, and then carried him over to the side of the road. Calmly, his savior assured him that help was on the way, and then left. He never saw the man again. I felt this was a story waiting to be told but from the rescuer's vantage point.

I had a sister living on Bainbridge Island at one time, and loved the ferry ride over to visit her, so I added that location for color in the story. If you have never taken that ride or visited Bainbridge, put it on your to-do-list.

Because don't we all fantasize about a three-button lunch or a five-button dinner?

The Clock Changer

It was a typical fall day in New York City. Typical for everyone except three people who would collide in a subway station and share an unforgettable evening.

Robert Engle checked his watch again. Noon. Work wouldn't be expecting him for another three hours, but today he was too anxious to stay at home. He wanted to be out and moving. Anything to soothe his nerves.

"Calm down, Robert," his wife Michelle said. "There is nothing more we can do. Now it's up to fate."

If anything, the words increased Engle's agitation and got him pacing even faster in their small house. The sight of their wall phone brought him to a halt. He dialed a well-remembered number.

A young feminine voice answered. "Hello?"

"Hi, sweetie. How are you doing?"

"I'm fine, dad. Aren't you supposed to be at work?"

"No, I go in later today. Tonight is when we turn the subway clocks back."

The girl laughed. "In this modern day, don't those clocks adjust themselves?"

"Most do, but the sixty- to seventy-year-old clocks still need to be changed manually."

"So what are there, ten or fifteen of these old ones?"

"Try 250."

"Wow. And you're supposed to have them all changed by two am?"

"Yeah, hubs like Rockefeller Center have twenty-four of these old clocks. West 4th Street, my last stop for tonight, has eighteen." He realized he was babbling. "How are the kids?"

"Constantly causing trouble except when they're asleep," she said.

"Since all seems quiet, I guess they're sleeping."

"At least for now. Oh, are we still getting together for dinner tomorrow night? And what is this big event you want to celebrate?"

The question caught him by surprise, and he tried to keep the stress out of his voice as he replied, "You'll find out."

"Uh, oh. The kids are already up. Got to go. Love you, dad."

"I love you too, honey," he said to a dial tone.

Five minutes later, he was starting out the door when his wife caught him by the arm. She held out a small paper bag. "You almost forgot this."

Engle carefully took the bag and shook his head. Tonight he couldn't afford to make mistakes.

When Christopher Miller glanced up at the wall clock, it also was noon. Although it was a Saturday, he'd been in the office now for four hours, and still had stacks of work demanding his attention. When he had graduated from law school, the chance to work at Campbell, Schwartz, and Lennon had seemed like the opportunity of a lifetime. But in order to get that chance, he had given up most of the hours that comprise a lifetime outside of the office. And trying to stay ahead of the work was nothing compared to competing with the other associates, all trying to maneuver up the corporate ladder.

Oh, well, he told himself for the umpteenth time, long-hard-hours were the life of the new associate lawyer in a big firm. He was making good money, shared a nice apartment, and lived in the city that never slept. What more could he ask for? How about a life outside of the office, he replied to himself. That would be nice. Even more so, how about a girlfriend? Now that would be really nice. And hopefully, tonight might be a small move in that direction.

A dark haired young man, dressed in Saturday causal, dropped into one of the office chairs.

"Hey, I heard you're going to old man Campbell's holiday party tonight with One Strike," he said.

Chris pointed to the stacks of files on his desk. "I don't have time for joking, Barry." He picked up his pen and started back on his work, only to drop it a few moments later, and lean back in his chair. "Okay. I'll take the bait. Who is One Strike?"

Barry grinned. "You didn't think Campbell's daughter asked you out because of your looks? Or your future earnings?"

"I don't know. Thought she might have some good reason."

"Let me guess how it happened. Old man Campbell's secretary called you and set the date up, right?"

"Yeah, so what?" Chris said impatiently.

"Have you ever met Campbell's daughter?"

"No, but I've seen pictures of her. Pretty nice."

"Pretty unattainable is what she is." Barry glanced around the room, and lowered his voice. "Her father has her take some of the new promising associates to the office parties throughout the year. Word has it she grades them and reports back to him."

Chris looked over. "And she got her nickname, why?"

"She never goes out with the same associate twice, never! Hence the nickname 'One Strike and You are Out'." He snickered. "We just call her One Strike."

Leaning back in his chair, Barry said, "Did you do some work for her father lately?"

"Yeah, I did all the ground work for the Tippman deal."

Barry nodded. "That was a sweet piece of lawyering. And that's why he sic'd his daughter on you. Wants to know you better."

Chris crumbled up a piece of paper and threw it across the room. "I finally get a date in this town, and it turns out to be a job interview."

"Oh, I haven't told you the best."

Chris swung toward him. "Which is...?"

"Well, since the best studs in this firm have gone down in flames against her, the rumor is that she's gay."

At the same time, Susan Campbell pulled the blanket off her head, and with one eye open, saw that her bedside clock read noon. Way too early, she thought as she yanked the blanket back over her head. She'd been up until four a.m. finishing an article for *Woman's World*. It had finally reached the rewrite point of where they-could-take-it-or-leave-it, and she had emailed it in. Her next article for *Vogue* wasn't due until next week, so today was going to be her day to kick back, relax, and...oh, crap! Her father's office party was tonight. Damn, damn! She had sold her soul to the devil when she borrowed that money from her dad to make the down payment on her apartment. He kept coming up with all sorts of little chores she could do for him as payback. And tonight was another of his ridiculous tasks.

She climbed out of bed, made a brief stop in the bathroom, and then shuffled off to the kitchen.

"Thank God for automatic coffee makers," she said aloud. She was adding cream to her cup when the phone rang. The caller ID showed it was her father. She thought about ignoring it but knew he would just keep calling.

She picked up the phone. "Hey, dad."

"Did I wake you, Princess," he said sarcastically. One of her cardinal sins, he repeatedly reminded her, was sleeping in and letting the morning go to waste.

After a sip of coffee, she said, "No, just got back from a six-mile run. How are you this morning?"

"I'm tying up loose ends regarding the party tonight." He paused. "You haven't forgotten that you are going with Christopher Miller tonight?"

Susan said nothing. She waited for him to pull out his usual reminder, and she wasn't disappointed.

"How's the apartment doing? Still enjoying the location?"

Shaking her head in resignation, she said, "Yes, the apartment is great and thank you for your help. And no, I haven't forgotten about my date tonight." Might as well stick it to him. "And no, I don't have anything to wear, nor shoes to wear it with. And my nails are a mess, and my hair a fright. So can I borrow your credit card?"

Her father's laughter boomed through the phone. "No question whose daughter you are. You would have been a hell of a lawyer. Still not too late."

"Thanks, dad, but that's not for me." She hesitated a moment. "And this is the last time I go on a date with one of your associates."

"Susan, your impressions of them are very helpful to me."

"Cut the crap, dad. I know why you keep forcing me into these dates. Please understand that I can find a husband without your help, and he is never going to be a lawyer. So after tonight I am done, and don't think bringing up the apartment will change that."

After they hung up, she walked back into her bedroom to check her outfit for the night. The dress and shoes were already pick-ed out, but she did need to get her nails and hair done. Her eyes lingered on the words of her favorite wall poster.

"Late at night I toss and I turn and I dream of what I need. I need a white knight upon a fiery steed."

As if there were one of those on this asphalt-covered island, she thought as she began preparing for the day.

Robert Engle stood on his ladder in Rockefeller Center, at eye level with the wall clock. Normally, he worked as an MTA con-tractor installing and maintaining billboards throughout the subway system, but two days a year he was in charge of changing the older subway clocks for daylight savings time. Tonight was one of those days.

With a practiced motion, he loosened and removed the screws holding the faceplate of the ancient clock. Checking the exact time with his cell phone, he then manually adjusted the clock back one hour. After a quick wipe of the clock face with a rag, he closed up the faceplate and screwed it back down. It was only 7:45 pm so he could relax. Reset four more of these and then he was off to the West 4th Street station clocks. And there, once his job was done, he could focus on the real purpose of this particular evening.

Chris Miller walked up the stone steps and entered into the brownstone's foyer. A glance at his watched showed 7:45 p.m.

Checking the tenant list, he rang the buzzer next to the name S. Campbell.

The voice over the speaker was muffled. "You do know you are fifteen minutes early, right?"

"Sorry, I just didn't want to be late," he said. "I'll wait down here until you're ready."

It was a moment before the muffled voice came again. "No, come on up. I'm in apartment 3B. The door is open. Help yourself to a beer. I need a few more minutes."

As with most of the old brownstones, there was no elevator so Chris trudged up the stairs to the door of 3B. It opened easily and he entered a modest sized combination living room-dining room with a small kitchen to the right. He heard the hair dryer going behind the closed door to the left. Wandering around, he saw a picture of a younger Susan on horseback jumping a fence. Another picture showed a more recent Susan sitting next to her father in the cockpit of a generous sized sailboat. He strolled into the kitchen and decided a beer might be nice. On the refrigerator door were multiple pictures of adults and kids in various poses and activities, with Susan in several of them.

Chris returned to the living room and dropped onto the couch. With each sip of beer, Chris found his apprehension lessening.

"Hello."

Startled, Chris turned at the sound and there she was framed in the doorway. He knew she was 31 years old, but looked younger. Long, honey blond hair contrasted nicely against her black, clinging dress, which highlighted a figure that should be highlighted. Startling bright blue eyes, not apparent in her photographs, were set in a pretty face.

He rose up and put out his hand. "Hi, I'm Chris Miller."

Slipping her hand into his, she replied, "Susan Campbell. Nice to meet you." She grabbed her coat off the couch. "Shall we get going?"

Chris took a last swallow of beer and then helped her put her coat on.

"You look very lovely tonight," he said.

Susan turned toward him. "I'm going to do you a favor, Chris, and be very honest with you."

"Please do."

"My father keeps setting me up with his junior associates in hopes I will find one to marry. But I have no intention of ever getting involved with a lawyer. Is that clear?"

Great way to start the night he decided, but since we are being honest. "Well, I had no plans to pursue you since I was told you prefer women."

She laughed. "And where did you hear that?"

"A rumor floating around the office." He paused and put his hands up in front of himself. "Now, don't get me wrong, I have nothing against being gay."

"Well, isn't that generous of you." She eyed him for a while. "Aren't you going to add the proverbial comment that some of your best friends are gay?"

What the hell he decided. I'm not going anywhere with this girl so why not pull her chain. "Actually, I had a date tonight, but when your father's secretary called and begged me to take you out, I reluctantly cancelled."

Susan regarded him for a long moment. ""Why don't we start over? I didn't mean to take my frustration with my dad out on you."

"Sounds good to me."

Extending her hand, Susan said sweetly, "So nice to meet you, Chris. And I prefer men."

Chris shook her hand and gave her his best smile. "You look very lovely tonight."

With a shake of her head, and a polite smile, Susan said, "Thank you. And you look very nice yourself."

"I hope so since this is the only decent suit I own. And by the way, my date was a guy. We were going to a ball game."

They stared at each other, and then both laughed.

This could be an interesting night thought Chris, enjoying the sound of her laugh.

Susan led the way down the stairs with Chris behind keeping up a one-sided conversation.

"Nice apartment. Perfect for one person. Mine's somewhat smaller, and I share it with two other lawyers."

They were nearly down to the first floor when Susan said, "I was in the same situation, except sharing with three girls. My father loaned me the down payment for this place. It wasn't until later that I discovered his generosity came with strings."

"Like taking out wet-behind-the-ears junior associates?"

She was happily surprised that Chris understood and could easily joke about her father's intentions behind these office dates. Already he was not the usual date her father had shoved on her. In the past, her father's dating merry-go-round had been law geeks, social cripples, or egotistical blowhards. The only decent ones seemed to be trying to impress her merely to win favor with her father. Chris didn't fit in any of these categories... at least not so far.

It was late, in fact 1:40 a.m., yet Robert Engle was anything but tired. He had waited fifteen years for tonight and he was wired with adrenaline. He had only one more clock to turn back at the West 4th Street station, but it was key in tonight's activities. He opened the clock's faceplate, and left it like that as he climbed back down the ladder, and began the waiting. He noticed his hands were shaking with anticipation.

The Campbell, Schwartz, and Lennon office holiday party was always held in Albert Campbell's magnificent apartment set high above the East River. It was the premier event of the season for the law firm. Even the lowest law clerks cleared their calendar for this gathering. The food was gourmet, the liquor top drawer, and the music a perfect mixture of old and new classics. And as an added bonus, the younger members had a chance to rub elbows with the heavy hitters in the firm, and maybe strengthen working relationships with them.

By 1:30 am, the party had finally started to break up, and couples were slowly leaving. Susan's father, Albert Campbell, walked Chris and Susan to the door.

"I'm really happy you both came tonight. I think this was one of the better parties we've had. A bit crazy, but nothing that should result in divorce."

They all laughed.

"You and mom did good, dad," Susan said, giving him a hug. "Everything was perfect."

Chris helped Susan into her coat, and said, "Mr. Campbell, this was a great party. Thank you very much for inviting me."

"My pleasure, Chris. And please, call me Albert."

Campbell ushered them out the door. "Be safe," he said. "I'll talk with you tomorrow Susan."

"Not before noon, you won't," she replied.

"Oh yes, I forgot. Call me after your six-mile run," he said with a wink.

They walked down the hallway to the elevator where Chris

checked his watch. 1:40 am. "I can't believe it's this late," he said. "Thank God tomorrow is Sunday."

Susan adjusted her coat. "Actually, it's not that late. Remember we turn back the clocks tonight."

Chris hit his forehead with his palm. "I not only forgot that but I didn't thank your dad for arranging this date."

"So you had a good time?"

"Very nice, surprisingly."

"Surprisingly?"

After pressing the elevator button again, Chris said, "As you may remember, the night didn't start so smoothly."

"Well, I think once we got my sexual preference settled, it seemed to get better."

Smiling, Chris leaned against the wall. "I saw ten guys in there that couldn't keep their eyes off of you. And the looks I got for being with you made me afraid to turn my back for fear of getting knifed."

Susan laughed. "I thought all lawyers looked at each other that way. Isn't a knife in the back considered de rigueur?"

"Since my French sounds like Peter Sellers doing Inspector Clouseau, I'll limit my reply to English. Yes."

The elevator arrived and they stepped in. Chris began scanning the elevator buttons.

"Try the down button," she offered with a laugh. "That usually does the job."

"Well, aren't you the big city girl," Chris responded.

In less than seven minutes, they had reached the West 4th Street subway station, and were down on the platform. According to the service board, the uptown train wasn't due for another ten minutes. They walked past the magazine-food kiosk, and waited at the edge of the platform.

Susan walked over to one of the clocks, and stood beneath it. "Chris, can you take a picture of me here? I want to show my girlfriend that on occasion I do stay out late at night."

Chris maneuvered her into a good position and snapped a picture with his cellphone. "I'll text you a copy," he said.

They were moving back to the edge of the platform, when Susan abruptly stopped. "Darn. I just got something in my eye," she said, putting her finger up to the edge of her right eye. As she was gently manipulating it, a passerby bumped into her right arm.

"Oh, my God," she said pulling back, "I've dropped my contact."

Chris glanced at her eyes and noted one was still bright blue but the other was now green. "Do you have blue or green eyes?"

She bent over, examining the ground around her. "I have one of each. It's called heterochromia."

"Hey, that's pretty cool."

"Yeah, for an Australian Shepard. Tinted contacts saved my life." She crouched lower and tilted her head, trying to get a better view along the cement surface.

Chris immediately picked-up on her vulnerability, and the importance of the contact. He motioned several people back while they combed the ground.

"Oh, damn," Susan said, pointing over the edge of the platform.

He looked down at the tracks and initially saw nothing. Getting down on his knees and leaning over, he finally saw the lens laying on top of the metal rail.

"How did you ever see that?" he said. "Give me a second, and I'll have it for you."

She grabbed his arm. "Don't even think of it. People get killed all the time trying to get things that have fallen on the tracks."

He slipped out of her grasp. "It will only take a second. Hey, the next train's not due for another eight minutes." And with that he jumped from the platform down amongst the tracks. Cautiously, he bent and lifted the contact lens off the track, turned and handed it up to Susan.

"See, no big deal."

"Thank you, now get out of there before something happens," she urged, glancing expectantly down the train tunnel.

Chris put his hands on the platform which was about mid-chest height. He was preparing to swing up, when a man offered him his hand. With a quick jerk, he pulled Chris up onto the platform.

The man was older, probably mid fifties, with a thick waist, gray hair, and muscular forearms. He was wearing a green uniform with an MTA patch on the shoulder.

"Thank you," Chris said.

The man smiled at Chris and put out his hand. "I'm Robert Engle."

They shook hands, and Chris said, "Chris Miller, and thanks again."

"You're welcome." He started to turn away, and then said, "Is it possible you could help me with something," he said. "It will only take a few minutes."

Chris glanced over at Susan who shrugged her shoulders in a why-not gesture.

"Well, we're waiting for the next uptown train," Chris said.

"Not a problem. It won't take that long."

"Okay," Chris said. "What do you need?"

Engle hesitated and then said, "It might be easier to show you. I'm the clock changer so let me turn back this very last clock," Engle said. "It's 1:57am, and I'm supposed to have every clock turned back before two a.m."

"You change every clock in the subway?" Chris asked, as he and Susan followed Engle down the platform.

"I have others that help, but I am the main man," Engle said climbing a ladder set under the clock. He pointed toward a green elevator that was further down the tracks, just past the kiosk. "I'll meet you there."

Susan and Chris slowly drifted down the platform to the elevator. In less than a minute, Engle appeared and ushered them into the open elevator. Moving to the control box, he screwed a flashlight-sized metal handle into a socket on the box. There were a number of knobs on the handle which he carefully adjusted.

"Hang on," he said, as he pressed the down button and the doors closed.

Chris and Susan glanced at each other. Lifting her eyebrows, she mouthed, "Hang on?"

There was a feeling of motion, like someone was shaking the elevator itself, along with a whirling sensation, and then everything went still. When Engle opened the door, Susan and Chris found they were still on the same platform. Nothing appeared to have changed except now there were more people present.

Engle pointed toward the Kiosk. "Go check the newspaper and tell me the headline story."

"What?" Chris asked.

"Check the paper."

Chris and Susan walked to the newspaper stand and picked up a newspaper. Across the banner in big letters: "Bush Defeats Gore to Win Presidency." Half-way down the front page, they spotted a smaller headline: "Hilary Clinton Elected NY Senator."

Chris checked the date of the paper: Nov 8th, 2000.

Susan tapped his arm and pointed to a glass display which held a movie poster: Meet the Parents. "That came out in 2000," she said, "on my sixteenth birthday."

Chris gestured to the clock that Engle had been adjusting. The time now was 8:14pm.

They rushed back to the elevator.

"What's going on?" Chris says. "Is this a trick, a joke, what?"

"It's not a trick, but I had to demonstrate it before I tried to explain or you would never have believed me."

"You mean believe that you had taken us back 15 years in time?"

"Just hear me out," Engle said. He pointed to the clock he had last adjusted. "When I turned the time back on that last clock to one a.m., it created a continuous doorway into the past. A doorway that remains open until that clock catches back up to 2 a.m."

"There is no such thing as time travel," Chris said empathically.

Engle stretched his arms and said, "Imagine time is like a long sheet of paper rolling into a machine that records time on the paper, and stores it for posterity. When we turn back the clock, we are pulling a short length of that paper back out of the machine. This segment has come into contact with all the recorded pages of time sitting in the machine. When we pull that limited bit of paper back out, it is our gateway into the past until it once more enters the machine. So too, when we turn the clock back, it gives us that short opening into the past."

"This is absolutely crazy," Susan said.

"It's the best explanation I've have come up with," Engle

replied. "And over the years, the only one that makes sense... at least to me."

"How does this elevator work? And that device you plugged in, what's that?" Chris asked.

"I can explain later when we have time. Even I don't know exactly what makes it work, but it can carry you back to any moment in the last fifty years. There are two limitations. You can only do this on the evening we set the clocks back. And you only have one hour in that time space before the paper straightens itself out and you are pulled back into the present."

"Why are we at this particular day and hour?"

"There is something that needs to be done for which I need your help."

Susan stepped between Chris and Engle. "If you wanted something done in the past, why not go there and do it yourself?"

"I did, but whenever I tried to leave the elevator, everything would immediately revert to present time. And then I realized that only you could do it."

"We've never even met before. How would you know I am the one to do whatever it is?" Chris demanded.

Glancing at his cell phone, Engle looked up and said with obvious urgency, "You have only 55 minutes left before that clock hits 2 am, and we are returned to present time."

"What is this thing that only I can do?" Chris said.

"Right now, there is a young girl named Reagan on the second level of the Brooklyn Bridge who is going to commit suicide. You need to talk her out of it."

It was several more moments before Chris spoke. "You're kidding, right?"

Susan slowly shook her head in disbelief.

Stepping in front of the elevator exit, Engle said, "You're stuck in this time zone for another 55 minutes. What if I am right and you are the only ones that can save her life tonight. Not only save her, but help all the people whose lives her death will affect."

He saw the hesitancy in their eyes. "If there was any other way I would have done it long ago. You are my last hope."

Chris and Susan exchanged looks. Chris finally shrugged his shoulders and said, "This just keeps getting crazier and crazier."

Engle clapped him on the back. "You only have 53 minutes so you need to hurry."

It was several moments before Chris spoke, "Okay. We'll see what we can do."

After a few instructions, Chris and Susan raced up the stairs, and out onto the street.

As he watched them go, Engle made the sign of the cross and said softly, "And be very careful."

When they reached the street, Susan grabbed Chris' arm. "We need to stop and think about this whole thing. It's just too bizarre to be real. Don't you think so?"

"Hell, I don't know what to think. But if he's right, and some girl's life is in our hands, we need to get there as fast as possible."

Susan glanced around getting her bearings. "The Brooklyn Bridge is that way, about a mile or so. We'll never find a cab this time of night."

"Must be some kind of omen," Chris said pointing down the street. "There's an empty cab."

They raced to it and as they climbed in, Chris yelled, "Brooklyn Bridge as fast as you can. Get us there in less than 10 minutes and I'll triple the fare."

After searching his pockets, Chris leaned into Susan, and said quietly, "Do you have any money?"

"This is why I never date lawyers. They are always taking other people's money."

The cab roared down the street, screeched around several corners, and came to a sudden stop at the bridge entrance.

The cabbie looked back over his shoulder. "Seven minutes flat, Bub."

After paying the driver, they turned toward the huge imposing structure that was the Brooklyn Bridge. In the misty, darkness, it appeared like an apparition from 19th century London. At one time it had been called the "Eighth Wonder of the World" since it was the longest suspension bridge of its time.

There were two tall, granite towers at either end built in the East River. The towers were connected by thick steel, suspension cables draped between them, running on either side of the bridge.

"I'm not sure where to start searching," Susan said, looking at the first level of the bridge which had three lanes of traffic going in each direction.

"Engle said she's on the second level," Chris replied. He pointed at the pedestrian walkway, centered on the bridge, which formed the second level and was about two car lanes in width. "That means we go there."

Susan pulled off her shoes, and they both began to run. There was just a scattering of people strolling on the walkway which they easily avoided, even in the dim light. Several turned to see what the rush was all about.

"Engle said she was past the first tower and on the left side, although how he knows is anyone's guess," Chris said, breathing rapidly. "Damn, these suits are not made for running."

"Try bare feet and a dress," Susan shouted back.

They had just passed the first large stone tower, when Susan stopped. "There she is," she said, pointing toward the edge of the bridge.

Chris picked out a dark, huddled figure sitting on a steel beam that ran along the edge of the bridge at the same height as the walkway. She had her arm wrapped around a support cable while her feet dangled out over the edge of the beam. It was not surprising that no one had seen her. With her black coat against the night sky, she was nearly invisible.

They moved to the metal fence at the edge of the walkway.

"What was her name? Riley?" Chris said as he was buffeted by a gust of wind.

"No, Reagan."

Chris cupped his hands and yelled. "Reagan, Reagan." The girl never turned.

"She didn't hear you," Susan said.

"It's the traffic noise and the wind." He looked around. "I need to get closer."

Within seconds, they realized the only avenue to get closer was to crawl out on one of the metal girders which extended out from the pedestrian walkway and connected to the beam Reagan was sitting on. Unfortunately, these same metal girders ran just above three lanes of busy traffic. A fall would be near certain death by the cars below.

Susan latched onto Chris' lapel. "You're not going out there. Try calling her again."

Yelling as loud as he could, Chris said, "Reagan, we are here to help. Let's talk about this."

This time the girl half turned and saw them. She answered something but it was lost in the noise.

"I've got to go out to her," Chris said. "Just wish I wasn't afraid of heights."

"Wait!" Susan demanded, pulling out her cell phone. "Let me call 911. They can be here within minutes."

"These types of cell phones weren't even invented fifteen years ago so good luck making a call."

"I'll find someone to make the call. You just stay here." She spun and ran toward one of the walkers. "There's a girl trying to commit suicide. Call 911," she yelled at the walker.

He looked perplexed. "Where?"

Susan turned and pointed toward Reagan, and at that moment saw Chris starting to crawl out on one of the girders.

Susan had just left to get help when Chris saw Reagan make a movement toward the edge of the beam. She's getting up her courage to jump, he realized. I don't have time to wait for the police to get here. He swung a leg over the fence and stepped onto the girder. The proximity to the river had put a fine mist along the girder surface making it wet and slippery. He got down on his knees.

Son of a bitch. It's not enough I'm crawling out over the racing cars, but my safe haven will be a narrow piece of metal suspended hundreds of feet in the air. He started feeling that sense of vertigo he got with heights; a feeling like he was being pulled toward the edge and was going to fall no matter what he did. It created a paralysis in his mind and his muscles. Closing his eyes, he focused on the sound of the traffic using it as white noise to quiet the scream of fear deep within his subconscious.

"Now I'm going to open my eyes, and just look straight ahead," he said loudly to make sure his mind heard the command. "I will not look down!"

When he did open his eyes, he saw Reagan still perched on the edge. She hadn't moved any farther. He began to slowly crawl out on the beam. He was half way across when his right knee slipped off the edge. As he started to fall, he wrapped his arms and both legs around the beam and hugged it as tightly as possible. Above the traffic noise and distraction of car lights, he heard Susan yelling for him not to move, that the police would be here soon.

There was no way he could remain where he was, dangling above the steady traffic, without becoming completely panicked. Cautiously and deliberately, he got his knees back up on the beam and began once more to inch forward. The earth was created in less time than it took for him to reach the cross beam that Reagan was seated on, grab the suspension cable she was holding, and swing his legs over so he was sitting next to her with the cable between them.

"Go away. Leave me alone," she said.

"I'm here to help you, Reagan."

"What? To help me jump?"

"No, to talk you out of this." Chris took a glance down which caused him to clutch the cable even tighter.

"Who are you? How do you know my name?" she said.

"I'm a friend. Looks like you could use one right about now."

Much earlier the same day, Reagan had stood in front of her bathroom mirror getting ready for school. She wondered why God had been so unkind to her in the looks department. Naturally curly hair while everyone else's was straight. Braces and glasses. Too heavy. Acne that wouldn't go away. And no sense of fashion, which really didn't matter, since her parents couldn't afford to buy her the "right clothes" anyway. In fact, they could barely afford the private school she attended. At least in class, she was an academic star, but everywhere else she felt like a social loser.

Picking up her coat and backpack, she paused at the doorway dreading what lay ahead in her day. For some reason, she had become the target of several of the "in-crowd girls," and each day was becoming more and more unbearable.

"Hurry up, honey, or you're going to be late," her mom yelled from the kitchen. "Your dad and I have a dinner plans with friends tonight so we won't be home until 9."

Glancing out the window, she noticed the drizzle. Great. Her hair was going to be even more frizzy than usual. Under the cover of an umbrella, she hurried to the subway and caught the train for school.

Her morning classes were a breeze today, and she enjoyed the chance to show what she knew.

She met her best friend, Alice, in the school cafeteria for lunch. Reagan was discussing her day in class when Scott Parker and two of his football teammates approached the table.

Reagan had tutored Parker through algebra and English, and if truth be told, had basically done all the work for him. She had developed a silent crush on him and who wouldn't have. He was the star quarterback, handsome, funny, but unfortunately in love with himself.

"Hey, Reagan. I heard a rumor you were hoping I might ask you to the winter ball." He winked at his two friends. "I don't want people to think that I would date someone that looks like you. Bad for my reputation."

"Stick you reputation up your ass," Alice said.

Parker snickered and spoke to his friends. "Do you think either of these two losers has ever been on a date?" Laughing, they all walked away.

Reagan grabbed Alice's arm. "Did you tell someone how I felt about Scott?"

Alice shook her hand off. "Maybe I mentioned it to someone. I don't remember. Hey, what's the big deal? Half the girls in school have crushes on that jerk, so you're just one more on the list."

"I thought I could trust you," Reagan said picking up her food tray, "or I never would have told you."

Other people in the cafeteria had heard the exchange with Parker, and the story spread everywhere. In her classes, Reagan would look up and see people pointing at her or staring at her. It was as if she was the brunt of a joke enjoyed by the whole school. And she knew what they were saying. Who did this little dweeb think she was, expecting Scott Parker to take her to the prom?

After school, she went to a nearby Starbucks. She did school work for several hours, and then pushed the books aside. Who was she kidding opening the books? Her life was a joke. And worst of all, that asshole Parker was right. She had never been on a date, and wouldn't know how to act if she got one. One girl had called her a frizzy haired, butterball with glasses, and that was who she was. Only she didn't want to go through life as that person anymore.

Picking up her books, she decided to walk home. That would take her by the Brooklyn Bridge. Her father had introduced her to the Bridge so many years ago. It was one of his favorite spots and he took her there frequently as she was growing up. She had grown to love the Bridge and often went there when she wanted to be alone or inspired. She loved the view of the city, the lights, the action, the promise of adventure and excitement, and it reaffirmed her connection with her father.

Walking out on the pedestrian pathway, Reagan found it cold, windy, and damp. This only added to her depression. It seemed like even the bridge had deserted her as a friend. Everyone would be happier without her, and in fact, she would be happier without them; without the constant torment and cruelty thrown at her day after day.

Before she consciously realized what she was doing, she found herself sitting on the metal girder, feet dangling over the edge, and arm wrapped around one of the support wires. It came to her then that it would be so easy to change everything. All she had to do was stand up and jump. Even she could do that. And then she had heard a voice calling her name.

"Leave me alone," she had shouted back. But now here was some stranger sitting next to her, offering to be her friend.

"What's so bad that you want to end your life?" Chris said, settling down on the ledge. Feeling an uncomfortable bulge in his back pocket, he pulled his cell phone out and set it on the ledge between them.

"I don't want to talk about it. Enough to say that my life at school is hell."

"If your time in high school is anything like mine was, then I totally understand," Chris replied.

"I don't need someone patronizing me."

"No, those four years were so bad that if there had been a bridge this size around, I might have contemplated jumping myself."

Reagan made no response. She just sat with her eyes closed and tears running down her cheeks.

Chris softened his voice. "I was a complete outcast. Embarrassment and clumsiness were my middle names. I'll never forget rushing into a bathroom stall only to realize, when I heard female voices that I was in the girls' bathroom. Took a long time to live that one down."

Very casually, Chris glanced back down at the street. No sign of the police yet. "And I was Mr. Awkward around girls. At the school parties, they wouldn't dance with me unless I took my shoes off since I stepped on everyone's toes. And of course, someone stole my shoes at one of the parties, and I was forever, 'Shoeless Chris'."

Reagan sat silent and then asked, "Did you ever have a date in high school?"

"Now you're really getting personal here." He ran his hand over his face. "No, but I came close. I was madly in love with the girl who sat in front of me in my English class. Before I got up the courage to ask her out, she started going steady with Jack McQuint, the coolest guy in school. And that was the extent of my dating life in high school."

Reagan looked over her shoulder, back at Susan. "Since you're with her, I guess things have gotten better."

"Realize that once you get out of high school and go on to college, a whole new world opens up. You can be anyone you want to be. People will judge you not on your looks or social status, but on who you are." Chris pointed to the lights of Manhattan. "That whole world over there is just waiting for you."

"It's too late. I can't go back now." Waving to the area she was sitting, she said "Once people find out about this, it will only be worse at school. And how could I face my parents?"

"Your parents would give the world to prevent this. And you can always change schools. Anything is possible, but you need to give it a chance."

She made no reply, and seemed to slide a bit further toward the edge.

"How about we make a deal," Chris said, trying to gain time until the police could take over. "We both go back. If your life still sucks this bad a year from now, I will meet you here and we can both jump together." He slapped the beam with his hand. "That's how confident I feel that things will be good by then."

Reagan made a violent shake of her head. "No! I want my life over now. It's too painful to go on, and too late to go back."

"Life is the greatest gift we've been given. What you do with it is up to you, not your schoolmates nor your teachers. In a year or two, you are off to college and you can become whoever you want."

Chris glanced quickly at his watch. He had only minutes left before his time was up. Suddenly, a loud voice, amplified by a bull horn, split the air. "This is the New York City Police Department. We are here to help you, young lady. Just sit tight and let us talk with you."

There was now a group of people gathered on the pedestrian walkway. On the street below, traffic was halted and multiple police cars with flashing lights were strewn across the roadway.

"Look at all those people that care about you and they don't even know you," Chris said. "And what about your parents? What will this do to them?"

Reagan stood, still holding the suspension wire.

"What are you doing, Reagan?"

"I want all this to be over. I should have jumped as soon as I got out here, but I was scared." She closed her eyes and took several deep breaths. "I appreciate you coming out here."

Chris saw a policeman climbing up the girder from the street, but he was never going to make it in time. There were also multiple officers on the street just below them.

With a grunt, Chris stood up. "Well, if that's the case and you're committed to jump, let me give you a pointer. Don't just step off; you need to leap away from the structure so you don't hit the bridge on the way down."

"Yeah, thanks… I guess." Reagan let go of the suspension cable, and flexed her legs in preparation to get a good leap away from the bridge. It was exactly what Chris wanted her to do. At that exact moment when she flexed her knees, Chris holding on to the same cable swung around in front of her. Letting go of the cable, he pushed her with both hands toward the safety of the policemen standing below.

Reagan yelled in surprise as she went backwards, but as she fell, one of her legs hit Chris' right leg and knocked it out from under him. He slipped, fell on the girder, and started to slip off. For a moment, his hand caught the edge and he thought he was okay, but then his handhold was gone, and he was free falling into the night.

After securing a 911 call, Susan had run back to the fence along the walkway. She'd seen his first near slip while he was crawling out over the traffic, and it was all she could do not to scream.

Over the next few minutes, a crowd gradually formed around her. She couldn't believe the direction the night had taken. Instead of a quiet subway ride home and kiss goodnight, they were in an episode of *The Twilight Zone*. She should never have let Chris go out on that beam. After what he did to get her contact lens, she should have known he'd do whatever needed to be done, and damn the risk. God, if something happened to him she would blame herself.

She saw Reagan stand, then Chris.

"She's going to jump," someone said.

They saw Reagan let go, and at that same instant Chris swing around and pushed her toward the outstretched arms of the police standing below. Susan started to shout with joy but the cry caught in her throat when she saw Chris slip. He managed to grab the edge of the girder and hang there for a few seconds. And then, he was gone from sight as she screamed.

Wham! His landing was hard, but Chris had heard that hitting the water from a height felt like hitting concrete. He was waiting for the water to close over him when he heard a voice.

"You okay?"

Chris opened his eyes and looked around. He was on the floor of the elevator. Susan was standing, her mouth agape, and it was Engle who had spoken and was now offering to help him up.

Seeing Chris' shocked expression, Engle said, "I told you when your time was up, you'd be yanked, and I meant yanked, back into the present. Fortunately, that pull came just before you hit the water." He put his hands on Chris's shoulders, and then hugged him. "You did good, son."

Pulling back, Chris said, "What happened? Is she okay?"

Engle paused a moment then with tears in his eyes, took out his wallet and removed a picture. The photograph was of an older Reagan with two young children. "Reagan is my daughter," he said. "When you saved her, you saved so many other people's lives. Now she's married to a great guy and has two gorgeous kids." Engle hugged Chris again. "I can't tell you what a hero you are in my family." Wiping his eyes, Engle picked up the paper bag his wife had given him earlier in the day and pulled the content out. "By the way, here is your cell phone."

Chris stared at it, and eventually said, "How did you get that? I left it on the girder."

"I've been holding it for 15 years, waiting for you to show up tonight."

"What?"

"After Reagan was saved, the police found your cell phone. They gave it to me thinking it was Reagan's. The cell phone's time and date didn't change when you went back in time."

"But how did you know that tonight I would be in this

particular substation?"

"There were pictures in the phone's memory. Reagan identified you in several of them, and thought she recognized the girl you were with in another photo. When I looked at that picture, I saw the West 4th Street station behind her and the clock just above her. So now I had the date, the time, the location, and pictures of both of you."

Susan shook her head. "Chris' cell phone was enough to figure this out?"

"It wasn't just the cell phone," Engle said to her. "Witnesses related that Susan had suddenly vanished, and, Chris, your body was never found. It was as if you both had ceased to exist. All that was left behind was a cell phone from the future."

"I still don't understand what lead you to an explanation," Chris said.

"I looked at the facts. Two people had come to my daughter's aid. The design and date on the phone belonging to one of them suggested that the phone was from the future, implying that these two people were also from the future."

"So you wondered who had sent them," Susan said.

"I figured it had to me," he said. "At the time, I was working as an MTA contractor installing and maintaining billboards throughout the subway system. I had heard an urban legend about a time continuum that could theoretically exist when the clocks were turned back in the substations."

"And when you saw that picture of Susan at the West 4th Street station taken just before the clocks were turned back," Chris said, "you wondered if the time continuum might be more than just legend."

"Exactly," Engle said. "I tracked down the head clock changer, and after much badgering, was finally able to get the truth."

"Which was?" Chris asked.

"That the legend was true. He hadn't wanted to tell me because he was afraid either I'd think he was delusional or worse, the whole story would get out. He had always been fearful of what might happen if the existence of the time continuum became public. He swore me to secrecy and made me a clock changer also. Over the years, I eventually became head clock changer and, with that position, guardian of the time continuum."

"And I thought *Star Wars* was far out," Chris said.

Engle nodded. "Anyway, my conversation with him allowed me to understand how Reagan had been saved, even though it seemed totally unreal. Since I knew the date and time you'd been in the station, and had pictures of both of you, all I could do was wait the fifteen years for you to appear."

"But what if I had failed to save her?" Chris said. "After all, anything could have happened to change the outcome."

"Don't you think I was aware of that? For fifteen years, I have watched my daughter evolve into the beautiful person she is, watched her get married and have children. All that time, I realized that if you failed tonight, everything would be erased." Engle shook his head. "It has been an unbelievable strain on my wife and me."

Chris clapped him on the shoulder. "Thank God you figured this out and she is fine."

"If you have this time travel ability," Susan said after a moment, "why haven't you gone back and changed other events?"

"Realize there are limitations - it places the person in this station, and they only get one hour - but even so, my predecessor tried it once. He sent his son back to November 21st 1963, and had him make a phone call from this station to the White House. He was treated as a crank call and they hung up on him."

"Oh, my God," Susan said. "President Kennedy was assassinated the next day."

"Think what might have been if someone had listened to him." Engle replied shaking his head. "So with that kind of failure, my predecessor never used it again. Besides, the travel handle - my metro card to time travel if you will - can only be used once every ten years. It takes that long for its power to be recharged, and for the tear it creates in time to be repaired."

"How does this handle work?" Chris said.

"No one knows," Engle said, looking at the time handle. "There is a rumor, and I stress rumor, that Albert Einstein in the early 1950's came to NY on several occasions, each trip just before the clocks where set back. He spent a lot of time in this station and, rumor again, specifically in this elevator. If anyone could have understood this time travel business, he was that man. And as far as I can determine, it was around then that the time handle showed up."

They all stood silently contemplating the incredible events of the night, and realized that no one outside of those involved would ever believe such a story.

"If you don't mind, I have one more favor to ask," Engle said shyly.

"No, I am done with time travel and saving damsels in distress," Chris said, cringing.

Engle laughed. "No, this is a bit easier. We are having a dinner tomorrow night to celebrate my daughter's rebirth. I want you both to come."

Chris and Susan wandered back onto the platform and both immediately stared up at the clock. It was 2:15 am.

"I can't believe all that has happened in such a short time," Chris said.

Susan linked her arm into Chris' and leaned against his shoulder.

"You don't have a fiery steed parked around here, do you?"

* * * * *

Author's Notes: I have always been fascinated by stories where someone goes back into the past to alter what will happen in the present, such as in the "Terminator" movies.

I recently read a newspaper article about the man who is responsible for changing all the old clocks in the New York subway system either moving their hands forward or backward for daylight saving's time. Here was a man, I thought, who could actually alter time. So I put those two observations together, added some mumbo-jumbo, and you just read the result.

I had actually never been on the Brooklyn Bridge so it took a lot of computer time to visualize the structure of the bridge, and where a jumper might launch from. Sadly, there actually have been a number of suicides from this bridge.

<u>*Hats - The Last Great Adventure*</u>

Being a reporter in New York City has its benefits. My press pass gets me front row positioning for every major event in the city and gives me backstage exposure to all the big name entertainers. You may see me on the floor at the Garden for the Knicks basketball games or rubbing shoulders with the Giants' football team at the New Meadowlands. But, unfortunately, it also comes with one big disadvantage, a thing called a deadline.

I do the usual assigned day-to-day news stories for *The New York Times*, but my main journalistic contribution is a weekly column in the Sunday edition called "Heart of the City." Every seven days it's my job to come up with some interesting, previously unexplored side story about living in the Big Apple. Having grown up in the city helps, since it gives me access to people from all sorts of backgrounds, but it still is a stretch trying to create a captivating column week after week. So far I had been lucky, and my column had actually gained a little notoriety. New York One, the local TV news station, has featured several of my stories. There are even a few taverns where my face will bring free drinks, not that these are upscale establishments, but a free drink is a free drink.

This week my luck was running three furlongs short. I had no story line, not even a glimmer of what to write. I had scoured all my contacts, inspected every appropriate magazine and newspaper, searched the Internet, and in a fit of panic, even read the check-out-line tabloids, but still no hint for my column. What made it even worse was I had been pushing my boss for a raise which I desperately needed to continue residing in this money-sucking vampire of a city.

With just twenty-four hours left, I found myself sitting in Starbucks trying not to dilute my morning four dollar cup of coffee with tears of woe. I noticed the constantly changing crowd around me - the guy cutting articles out of the newspaper, the two women talking fashion savings at the knock-off stores on Canal Street, the obvious lovers with heads close whispering sweet somethings. Maybe one of them had a story that would fill my column?

My gaze moved past the coffee house throng, through the picture glass window, and onto Columbus Avenue. Beyond the constant flow of passersby, there was a black suburban parked in a two-hour zone with a man unloading stainless steel racks. He was mid-sixties, wrapped in a fleece jacket, wearing glasses, and a leather bomber cap. After setting up the racks, he quickly filled them with all manner of headwear, from fedoras, trilbys, and flat caps to cloches, beanies, and toques - all in a multiplicity of colors.

I shook my head at the ridiculousness of attempting to sell fashionable hats on a street corner. So it was a shock when people began stopping and trying on the various hats. Men in suits and ties, ladies in fashionable dresses and expensive coats, women with children, guys with backpacks. And through this continually shifting crowd, the owner glided, positioning their hats, offering the use of hand mirrors, whispering compliments. This innocuous little soul was a fly-fisherman who had waded into this sidewalk river of humanity, and was casting out his lures, pulling in the most unexpected catches. People of all shapes and sizes were buying these hats. I was amazed, and more to the point, I sensed a possible story.

"Hi, my name's Mark Fleming," I told the hat salesman. "I write a column for the *Times*, and I was hoping to ask you a few questions."

The man looked me up and down. "The name's Max and I've got just the hat for you. Give you some respectability," he said reaching toward the rack.

I started to protest but he held up a hand. "Trust me. As a reporter you need some respectability."

We stared at each other for a moment, and then he grinned. "Hey, I'm yanking your chain." He paused. "Fleming? You the guy that writes that column 'Heartless City'?"

"Heart of the City," I replied. "How do you like it?"

"Never read it, but my wife does and she's always telling me that Mark Fleming says this or Mark Fleming says that. Jeez, I can't get through the Sunday sports section without hearing about your latest comments. Can't you move your column to Mondays?"

I let that ride. "I'm thinking about a story on why people buy hats."

"Cause their heads are cold or they want to look better." Max shook his head. "Guess it's going to be a short column this week."

"Come on, there must be more reasons than that." I prayed there were more reasons.

"Nah, that's about it. Now what happens to them after they buy the hats, that's something I have always wondered?" He saw my confusion. "You know, how it affects their lives."

CLICK. On went the light. There would be a column this week.

"Do you mind if I ask your customers a few questions after they buy their hats?" I said.

"No problem, as long as you don't interfere with my sales."

With that, he turned to a young lady fingering one of the caps.

He took it from her hand, and said, "No, that's not for you. I got one that would turn heads on the Riviera." Fitting a burgundy wool beret on her blond head, he handed her a mirror and stepped back. "That is you. The essence of beauty. Since I can't imagine anyone else in that hat, I'll take 30% off the price."

As she continued to check the hat in the mirror, the owner pulled a hat off the rack and moved over to a young man in a dark suit. "Here, try this fedora. I call it the Frank Sinatra model." He positioned it on the man's head. "Now if you can croon, we will really have something."

And so it went, a different patter for each individual.

"Here's my Indiana Jones hat, made for a man of adventure. And I can tell that's you."

"No wedding ring? Try this bell shaped, fitted hat, miss. It's called a cloche and that flamboyant bow in front means you're single and ready to mingle."

"My friend, with your tattoos and pea coat, a porkpie hat would complete your image. Think Gene Hackman in The French Connection. Tough, no bullshit."

Over the next thirty minutes, I selected three hat buyers to approach, explained who I was, and asked each the same question. "Can I call you this evening and see what affect, if any, buying a hat had on your day?" They were all happy to help with my story.

My first call that night was to Bart Josephson. My notes reminded me that he was in his late twenties, and had been wearing a smart, dark blue suit with a red power tie. He was on his way downtown for a job interview. It was an incredible position with a large brokerage house, and he knew everyone was after it. Bart wanted to believe in his chances, but with his mid-level resume, he felt it wouldn't happen. Having some time to kill, he'd stopped to browse. Next thing Bart knew, this little guy in the bomber hat was at his side.

"These hats aren't for you," the man had told Bart, moving him to a different rack. "A man like you, who radiates confidence, needs a hat that says the same thing." He snugged a black fedora down on Bart's head. "Now this is what's called a short brimmed fedora or a trilby. How do I know this hat speaks confidence? Sean Connery wore this model in his first five James Bond movies, and that man was confidence in capital letters."

Bart stared at his image in the hand mirror. Not bad, he thought, as the James Bond theme music began to resonate in the back of his brain. The more he looked, the more he saw himself seated in an Aston Martin, a bewitching young thing riding next to him, as he screeched around impossible curves in the Alps.

"I'll take it," he said. As he walked on to his appointment, he could feel his self-assurance exploding to the point he wondered if maybe the job was beneath him.

It was a rude drop back to reality when he got off the elevator on the 20th floor, and opened the office door for *Jameson and Myers Brokerage Firm, Established 1938*. The outer office was filled with young men in dark suits with power ties, either sitting or standing, obviously there for the same reason.

When the secretary finally called his name, the waiting room was empty. As he followed the secretary back, she kept stealing glances at him. He surreptitiously wiped his chin, ran his tongue along his teeth, and checked his fly.

She led him to an open doorway. "Mr. Crowley. This is Bart Josephson, your last interview."

The office was minimalist in décor with two chairs, a desk, and one filing cabinet. No pictures or plants. Mr. Crowley matched the office with his plain white shirt, narrow tie, and thick, black rimmed glasses. Never looking up from the papers on his deck, Crowley used his right index finger to direct Bart to an empty chair. Still reading, Crowley said, "Your resume appears to be rather mundane, Mr. Josephson. Is there anything I should know that's not written here?"

Hearing nothing but silence, Crowley glanced up. Bart saw a sudden change in his blasé expression, a flash of interest. It took Bart a moment to realize what he needed to add to his resume. After that, they talked for nearly thirty minutes and Mark got the job.

I was amazed. "What fact had you left out?" I asked him on the phone. "You use to be Donald Trump's right hand man?"

Bart laughed. "I told you that the secretary kept checking me out. Well, it was because I was still wearing my hat. I was so nervous that I had forgotten to take it off. Well, that's what I decided had captured Crowley's interest."

"And the missing bit of information in your resume?"

"I told him that I loved hats."

"And that was because..." I said.

"I noticed a fedora on top of Crowley's filing cabinet, and I went with it. I told him the fedora was my favorite hat. Remembering what the hat seller had told me, I regurgitated it to Crowley, things such as the fedora was the favorite of Prohibition gangsters and film noir detectives, that Bogart wore one in Casablanca, and that Gene Kelly used it as a prop in *Singing in the Rain*."

"What was Crowley's response?"

"Nothing, and then he asked if I liked fedoras so much, why was I wearing a trilby? I think he was testing me. Thank God for the hat man. I told him I was a James Bond fan. Turned out that

Crowley was not only a huge hat lover, but a big film buff. We talked hats - actually, he did all the talking about that - and old movies. He was really a pretty good guy. Apparently everyone's resume was about the same, but I was the only hat lover."

I tried to keep my excitement under control. This had the beginnings of a great story, not Pulitzer quality mind you, but more than adequate for my column.

My second hat buyer was Sean Jacob. According to my notes and my memory, he was a junior member of a large architecture firm. I thought this appropriate since he had been dressed like a young Frank Lloyd Wright with dark grey pants, white shirt with the sleeves cuffed up, and a dark sweater vest. He was on his way for a luncheon date with a woman from the firm and was early. While waiting for the signal to change, he had wandered over to the hat collection, and of course, Max had snared him.

"A hat defines the man," Max had said, coming up behind Sean. "The question is what definition do you want?"

"I'm not following you," Sean replied.

"What kind of statement do you want the hat to make?"

Sean pulled a black beret off one of the hat racks and put it on.

As Sean studied himself in a handheld mirror, Max said, "The beret should be worn pushed to one side. These were the traditional hats of the Basque Shepherds in the Pyrenees. They wore them for protection against the cold mountain winds."

Sean started to take the beret off, but Max stopped him. "That was in the 19th century. Now, they're just cool."

Once again, Sean began to remove the beret. Max put both palms up in a halting gesture. "Che Guevara and Fidel Castro during their insurgency years wore these as a revolutionary symbol. A sort of 'Out with the old, in with the new' statement."

Lifting the mirror up, Sean took another look. He liked the 'Out with the old, in with the new' concept. "I'll take it."

Sean had explained to me that he was fighting for the attention of a wonderful, young woman in his office, another junior member. Unfortunately, she was presently starstruck by one of the senior partners who had been asking her out. The guy, Arthur Pearson, was fashion incarnate. Every day, he was dressed in a meticulously pressed, three-piece suit, and probably had the pockets stuffed with cash. Sean figured he had little to no chance competing against this bastion of respectability and fortune. Maybe that was the reason he'd chosen the beret to show he was revolting against the old guard.

He'd managed to talk Pamela into a luncheon date. Well, not actually a date. What she'd agreed to was a work-lunch to discuss one of the projects they were both involved with, but Sean had hopes it might evolve into more. She'd told him she'd meet him at the restaurant.

Walking toward the restaurant, he couldn't help checking how the beret looked in every picture glass window he passed. It gave him a revolutionary, individualistic look. After about twelve window checks, he decided he liked it.

Arriving at the restaurant, he glanced around for Pamela. To his surprise, he spotted Arthur Pearson sitting at a table and Arthur saw him. He waved Sean over.

"Hi, Mr. Pearson."

"Hello, Sean, and please, call me Arthur. Pamela mentioned you two were meeting here for a work related lunch and asked me to join you."

Sean was debating whether to strangle Arthur with his Harvard silk tie or stab him with a table fork when he saw Pamela approaching.

"Hello, Sean. Sorry, I'm a bit late," she said, and then realized who was sitting at the table. "Arthur, I'm glad you could make it."

Arthur stood up, and bowed slightly. "The pleasure's mine."

She smiled. "I hope that neither of you mind that I brought a guest." It was then that they noticed the very small girl trailing behind her. "This is my niece, Jill. Her mother, my sister, had to go to a doctor's appointment and couldn't find a babysitter."

Jill was three years old with long, blond hair, and light blue eyes set in a cherubic face. The waiter brought a booster chair for her and placed it between Pamela and Sean.

Arthur and Pam started a discussion on a new material being introduced to the construction world. Sean had trouble following because Jill was jabbering in his ear. Finally, Pam silenced her by handing her a bread stick.

"I'm sorry, Sean," Pam said. "I know this isn't the lunch you had planned."

She had no idea how right she was.

Before Sean could reply, Arthur launched into a statement about the firm and some of its future goals. Pamela was entranced. Sean was nauseated.

Bored with sitting, Jill pointed up at Sean's beret. "Giv'me that," she said loudly, reaching out for it.

"Here, have this instead," Sean said, giving her another bread stick.

Jill pushed it away and pointed at his hat. "I want that!"

Pamela grabbed her arm. "Jill, that hat is not yours." She lifted a bag set next to her chair. "Let's see what playthings your mother sent with you."

Jill yelled. "I want the hat. I want the hat."

Disapproving stares started up around them since no one likes a side order of screaming kid with their lunch.

"She hasn't had her morning nap," Pamela explained. She began to rise. "I'll take her outside for a moment."

"Wait a second," Sean said. He pulled off his beret and held it out to Jill. Instantly, she stopped yelling and grabbed the hat. When she put it on, it covered her eyes which got a laugh from everyone.

"Sean, are you sure?" Pam whispered.

"Pam, it's only a hat."

Arthur turned to Sean. "I seem to have been monopolizing the whole conversation, Sean. You two were going to talk work, so don't let me interrupt." He stood up, walked around to Jill and slid her chair over next to him. After removing his coat, he squatted down to her level and said, "Jill, I have a wonderful story for you and it's all about a cat in a hat."

"Thanks, both of you," Pam said with evident relief. She swung back toward me. "Okay, let's talk about the Gunderson project."

Sean was too stunned to reply. This was not the Arthur he had envisioned. With a shake of his head, he managed to bring his focus back to Pam. There had been some minor sticking points regarding the Gunderson project. For the next forty-five minutes, as the food came and went, they brainstormed on what to do. Several times, Arthur tossed in helpful comments, but for the most part, he sat and listened, or skillfully guided Jill through her meal.

Pamela was exceedingly bright, but Sean had several years of field experience on her. The combination worked so well, that by the end of the lunch, they'd settled almost all of the structural questions. And by then, Sean had also settled the question of whether he had a chance with Pam. The answer to that was a very strong no! And if there was any further doubt, the adoring glances she periodically threw at Arthur answered that.

They walked outside and Sean flagged down a cab. Arthur helped Jill and Pam climb inside. After they drove off, Arthur and Sean opted to share a cab back to the office.

"Sean, I'm glad we had a chance to meet," Arthur said, settling back in his seat. "A lot of times, I just don't get a chance to interact with the junior members."

"It was a pleasure meeting you, sir," Sean replied.

"This lunch also gave me a chance to see what a smart decision we made hiring you. Your handling of the Gunderson project is quite ingenious."

"Oh, I think most of the credit goes to Pam. She is a super architect."

"I agree. She is very good, but she lacks your experience, and your ability to turn theoretical ideas into real possibilities."

"Thank you, Mr. Pearson," Sean said, trying to contain his surprise.

"Albert."

"Albert."

You know, I had a beret like yours once. It was in my Che Guevara days, when I was out to change the field of architecture." He smiled, seeing some distant memory. "I envisioned myself replacing old, archaic practices with new, exciting innovations." He looked over. "So when I saw that beret on you, it made me wonder if you too had that same burning, revolutionary spirit."

He stared at Sean for a long moment, and then clapped him on the knee. "We revolutionaries have to stick together, so how about joining me on a major project I am starting?"

As an avid card player, I knew that three of a kind was a great hand, so I prayed that my third hat person, Kelly Nix, had a story to match the other two. My short-hand scribbling told me she was a twenty-six year old graduate student, very cute (of course, that wasn't why I had picked her), who had been dressed in a long grey coat, wool scarf, short black dress, and boots to her knees. Max had talked her into a wool flat cap, which is a soft round men's cap with a small brim in front. Kelly remembered his exact words, "It denotes one of upper class who is affecting casualness." Not only did it match her scarf, but she had thought it made her more interesting.

Kelly had been on her way to meet an old acquaintance, a guy she hadn't seen since high school. It was her day off from work, so her plan was a quick cup of coffee with this guy, and then off to an evening play with her girlfriend.

"So how did the afternoon go?" I asked her, and she told her tale.

Kelly had gone straight to the Sensuous Coffee Bean on 72nd Street to rendezvous with her high school acquaintance. Looking around, there was no one that looked remotely like him. She wasn't sure why he had called her since they really had nothing in common. She'd been a Brainiac concentrating on going to college while he'd been a screw-around, always staying late for detention. If he hadn't been a star receiver for the football team, he would have flunked out. She knew the coach had personally paid for multiple tutors to help him make it to graduation, and she had been one of them.

Despite his shaved head, pimpled face, and scruffy beard, Kelly had seen the beginnings of a handsome man. And truth be told, his bad boy image also held some attraction. In addition, she'd seen a glimmer of intelligence when he wasn't clowning around, which gave her hope that she could bring him out of his intellectual apathy. But, it wasn't to be. His only ambitions had remained football and partying, to both of which he applied his full talents.

Wondering why they were meeting, she recalled their phone conversation.

"Kelly Nix?"

"Yes."

"This is Nate Christopher."

"I'm sorry. Who?"

"From Placerville High."

She remembered him now. "Oh, hi," she said cautiously. "How are you?"

"I'm doing fine." He paused. "I'm in Manhattan for few days and I was hoping I might get a chance to talk with you."

"Sure. What did you want to discuss?"

"It would be easier in person, say over a cup of coffee?"

They'd gone back and forth, but finally Kelly agreed with the meeting at the coffee shop. As she continued to look around, the guy was nowhere to be seen. She was starting for the door when someone stepped forward.

"Excuse me. Aren't you Kelly Nix?" The man was tall, with broad shoulders, Alpine blue eyes, slicked back hair, and clothed in a pinstriped suit. His tan was a sharp contrast to the alabaster color of everyone else in the room.

"Yes?" she replied. Who was this Adonis?

"It's me. Nate Christopher." His smile was an ad for the benefits of good dental care.

He held out a brown, manicured hand, enveloping Kelly's. Gesturing to a table in the corner, he said, "I have a spot for us. Would you like something to drink?"

There seemed to be something wrong with her tongue. It felt three sizes too large, and had no ability to form words. She finally stammered out, "Whatever you're having." Oh, great, she thought. How original.

"A non-fat, chai tea latte. That okay with you?"

Kelly made some vague nonsensical head motion in reply.

As he moved to the counter, she took in a long, slow breath. There is no way this God of fashion was that same crude football player. Just no way! This was some kind of a joke. That's it, she decided. One of my old high school friends is getting back at me.

Yet when he handed his money to the counter person, she saw a scar across the back of his right hand and winced. Yes, he was Nate Christopher for she had been the one that put the scar there.

It had been the third week of her tutoring and she'd been fed-up with his lack of attention, his buffoonery, and his continual flirting. She'd told him she was taking her tutoring book and going home. He tried to grab her book to keep her there. Antici-pating his move, Kelly had jabbed her pen down on the table top to block his hand. Underestimating his quickness, the pen ended up in the back of his hand, leaving a two inch laceration. She'd quickly wrapped her scarf around his hand and apolo-gized profusely.

She'd felt so guilty, she had continued tutoring him until the final exam. Shockingly, he passed the course, but she had re-fused to do any further tutoring. They'd never spoken again, and she could still remember his sudden quietness and haunted look whenever she had passed him in the school hallways.

"It has been a long time," Nate said. "You look great, but then you always did."

She sipped her tea, finally finding her voice. "Thank you, I appreciate that." After a pause, she added, "I truly didn't recognize you."

"Yeah, it always gets a laugh when people see my high school pictures." He smiled, and took a drink of tea.

"What are you doing these days?" she said.

He stared into his tea cup. "Well, that's why I'm here."

Uh oh, she thought, here comes the bad news.

"I'm sure you remember what a dullard, underachiever I was."

Kelly shook her head. "I remember a sweet, wholesome boy, only interested in learning." She maintained a straight face for a few seconds, and then both of them laughed.

"Yeah, right," Nate said." Well, I somehow managed to graduate and get a football scholarship to Colorado University. It took two years for me to realize I was never going to make the pros. I needed to think about another occupation, yet sports was all I knew." He took another sip of tea, his eyes in some distant memory.

"I called Coach Jackson, our old high school coach. After I explained my predicament, he told me he had a solution, but it wouldn't be easy, and I would owe him when it was all done."

He leaned back in his chair, and gently shook his head. "And he was right. It wasn't easy. When I wasn't on the practice field, I was in the library. After graduation, I went to law school."

"So you're a lawyer?"

"Not exactly. I got my law degree, and then I joined a firm of sports agents. With all my sports connections, it was a natural fit."

"That's wonderful."

After a prolonged pause, he said, "So what are you doing these days?"

"Interior design. I work for a small company in upper Manhattan."

"You always did have a sense of fashion," he said, and then looked up at her cap. "And that's a bold fashion statement."

"Hey, I was the high school's fashion guru or so I thought. Where else would I end up?" She paused, pushed her tea cup away, and leaned back. "Why did you look me up, Nate?"

"Payback to Coach Jackson. His deal was that I had to look up every tutor that got me through high school and thank them."

"I'm surprised you even thought of me. I only worked with you for six weeks."

"Well, it was enough. I passed the course." He hesitated, and then reached his hand across the table. "So I'm here to officially thank you."

Once again his hand enveloped hers, only this time he held hers a bit longer than before. As he let go, he glanced at his watch.

"I'm sorry, but I've got to get going," he said.

"What, another tutor to see?" she said mockingly.

"No, nothing like that." He rose up, his eyes on her cap. "It was great to see you, Kelly. I wish you the best of luck."

"It was good to see you too," she replied, somewhat shocked at his sudden departure.

He began to walk away, halted, and then turned back. "Coach told me to thank all my tutors, but you're the only one I met with face to face." He paused and then with startling intensity added, "You changed my whole life." Abruptly, he turned and walked out the door.

What was that all about, Kelly puzzled? First, he can't wait to meet with me, and now he can't wait to leave. She rose, walked over to the counter, and dropped her drink into the trash. "God, I hate chai-tea lattes."

Checking her watch, she decided she had more than enough time to get home and prepare for tonight.

"But what did he mean that I had changed his whole life?" she said loudly. There is no way that six weeks of tutoring did that. She remembered his comment about the boldness of wearing this hat. It must be true because she felt bold. And bold needed answers.

Darting out of the coffee shop, she searched both directions. On the other side of the street, at the end of the block, Nate was just disappearing into the subway entrance. Half running, she angled diagonally across the street into the subway entrance, then charged down the stairs. With a flick of her Metro card, she was through the turn-style. There he was, stepping into one of the subway cars.

Amazed at her audacity, Kelly ran and leaped into that same car just as the doors closed. She took a moment to catch her breath, and then glanced around, only to find Nate standing right in front of her with a shocked expression.

"What did you mean I changed your whole life?" she said.

Nate's expression changed from surprise to chagrin. After a brief hesitation, he said, "That day you injured my hand, I realized the incredible gulf that separated us." He paused. "Remember the book, *The Great Gatsby*?"

"The one I couldn't get you to read?"

"Well, eventually I did."

The train abruptly slowed and stopped, throwing her into Nate. His quick grab of both her and the support pole steadied them. Kelly quickly disentangled herself only to be crowded up against him when the doors open and more people packed the car.

As the train began to move, Nate leaned down and said, "I found myself identifying with Gatsby's obsession to raise his social position. I imagined myself standing with him as he gazed across the bay at the green light at the end of Daisy's dock. That light was his symbol of all that she was and all that he wasn't, but was hoping to attain."

Kelly found herself mesmerized by the way his lips formed his words.

"I remember looking at this scar," he said, lifting his right hand, "and it became my green light. A symbol of all the opportunities I'd ignored and all that I wanted to be. Whenever I felt like giving up, I would focus on this scar." He paused, looked away, and then back to her. "So that is why I wanted to thank you personally. Inadvertently, you gave me the push I needed when things seemed overwhelming."

"That's sweet, Nate."

The subway train made another stop, and but the car remained crowded, hemming them together. Kelly glanced up at him. "But couldn't you have just told me this on the phone?"

Nate took a deep breath, let it out slowly, and then leaned down and whispered into her ear. "I came to realize that the green light was actually you. The reason I had worked so hard was to become someone you might consider dating."

He straightened back up and stared into her eyes. Kelly held his stare for a long moment, then rose up on her tiptoes and whispered into his ear, "In a New York minute."

Nate gently put his arm around her and Kelly leaned into him. "If you wanted to ask me out, why make that remark then leave?" she said.

"It was your hat."

"My hat?"

"You have always intimidated me, and today was no different." He briefly glanced at her hat. "Now don't take this wrong, but I decided that if you had the courage to wear that funny looking thing, I should have the courage to ask you out."

Kelly's mouth dropped open.

"But after I made that comment about you changing my life," Nate said, "I lost my courage and fled."

It was a moment before she spoke. "You don't like my hat?"

"On you everything looks good, but that hat is stretching it."

Reaching into her bag, Kelly pulled out a pen. "Give me your right hand."

Nate yanked his hand back. "One scar is enough."

Kelly laughed. "I'm just going to write my phone number across your green light."

I had my story. It wasn't going to be about a man selling hats, or the type of people that buy hats, but rather the diverse and sometimes unexpected effects that wearing a hat could produce. I understood now that a hat affects not only the wearer, but also the world around them. In fact, it is an adventure to wear a hat since you never know what effects it might create. A hat could alter the wearer's self-image by creating confidence, improving one's sense of fashion, or heighten one's looks. A hat could also affect how the world perceived the wearer and interacted with them.

In the business world, a fedora combined with a Brooks Brothers suit would radiates style and success, but the same impressive suit worn with a baseball cap would fall flat. Yet at a baseball game, a suit with a fedora would look ridiculous, yet with a ball cap no one would look twice. There are so many un-expected impressions and reactions that come from simply placing these variously shaped coverings on our heads.

I spent the night writing and rewriting my article until it was tight. It was inspired journalism - or so it seemed at two a.m.

On the way to work, I stopped by my favorite hat stand. Max, in his fleece jacket and bomber hat, was busy hawking customers.

"Hey, Max, how are you?"

"Ah, Mr. Fleming. I told my wife I spoke with you yesterday. Suddenly, I'm a big man at home. Thank you."

"No, I wanted to thank you. Your question about what happens to these people after they buy their hats has given me a great column. And I'm hoping to do a sequel." I pointed to his hats. "I thought I might buy one for myself. What do you suggest?"

As I emerged from the subway station and headed for the New York Times building, I put my new hat on - a trilby. It was named after a hat worn in the London stage production of the 1894 novel, *Trilby*. It had been the playwright's favorite hat so it seemed appropriate headwear for a man who made his living with a pen.

The wind was gusting so I pulled it down tighter. Twice I stopped in front of store windows to admire my new appearance. Each time I liked what I saw - a jaunty, young man radiating style, grace, and confidence.

I was a block from the Times building when a sudden burst of wind caught the hat and blew it into the street. By the time I caught up with it, two cars had dragged and flattened it, and then the wind had blown it into a pool of stagnant water.

Bending down, I picked up the hat and brushed the water off the brim. Carefully, I tried to reshape it back into its once glorious appearance. I walked over to the plate glass window next to the Times entrance doors and put it on. The jaunty young man with grace and style was gone. In his place stood a bum in a crumpled hat.

I dropped the hat on my desk on the way to my editor's office. Through the glass panels, I could see Randy Charles sitting behind his desk shifting through papers. I entered and dropped my story on his desk top.

He glanced up. "I was beginning to think you had forgotten us."

"Ha, ha," I said without humor.

He slowly perused the pages, and then looked up at me. "Nice job, Mark. In fact, all of your columns have been very well done."

"Compliments are great, Charles, but they don't pay the rent."

He got up out of his chair, walked around to my side of the desk, and put his arm around me. "Thank God your writing is more original than your comments, Mark. I have decided, though, that you do need a raise."

"So my incredibly well written columns have finally gotten to you."

"No, it's because of your hat," he said distinctly.

"My hat?"

"Actually, it's the hat I saw you pull out of the gutter this morning as I was coming into work. I saw you clean it off and try it on. Now, I see that it's sitting on top of your desk. If one of my writers is so underpaid that he needs to select his clothing from the gutter, then it's time to give him a raise."

* * * * *

Author's Notes: The birth of this story was one of my more interesting adventures and it occurred just as described in the narrative. I was in New York, sitting in a Starbucks, trying to come up with a story idea. Nothing in the coffee shop was inspiring so I started to focus on the people walking by outside. I began watching this nondescript man set up a series of hat racks on the sidewalk and then start hawking them.

Wandering outside, I was caught up in his colorful sales spiels which were different for each potential customer. Several of his more creative enticements I actually included in the story. As I tried to think of how I could use his occupation for a story, I realized that it wasn't the hats that interested me, but rather the effect the hats might have on the buyer's life and so this tale was born.

While reading "The Great Gatsby," who didn't root for the underdog Gatsby to marry Daisy and live happily ever after. And who wasn't depressed with the eventual outcome. Haven't we all had a green light on some distant shore that we strived to reach and failed? So here was my chance to correct a literary disappointment that's bothered me since high school, and let Gatsby - Nate - finally have his Daisy - Kelly.

Stories for the Starving Romantic

The Author

T. J. Moran and his wife, Lydia, have lived in Carmel for more than 35 years. They have five grown children they are extremely proud of. And one yellow lab they aren't so sure about.

For more on T J, his stories, his forthcoming books, please go online to CarmelStories.com.

Other books from SetonPublishing.com

- by Tony Seton

13 Days of Fear

Mokki's Peak

Silent Alarm

Deki-san

Equinox

No Soap, Radio

Paradise Pond

Selected Writings

The Brink

Jennifer

The Francie LeVillard Mysteries - Vol I-IX

Trinidad Head

Dead as a Doorbell

Just Imagine

Musings on Sherlock Holmes

The Autobiography of John Dough, Gigolo

Silver Lining

Mayhem

The Omega Crystal

Truth Be Told

13 Days of Fear

The Quality Interview / Getting it Right
on Both Sides of the Mic

From Terror to Triumph /
The Herma Smith Curtis Story

Don't Mess with the Press / How to Write, Produce, and
Report Quality Television News

Right Car, Right Price

- by other authors

Sam The Morning Man - Sam Salerno
Hamilton & Egberta - Gerard Rose
A Dog's Tale - Ron Wormser
A Rich & Valued Life - Martin C. Needler
The Enchanted Emerald - Donald Craghead
The Dedicated Life of an American Soldier - Ray Ramos
Life Is a Bumpy Road - Tony Albano
From Hell to Hail Mary / A Cop's Story - Frank DiPaola
From Colored Town to Pebble Beach /
 The Story of the Singing Sheriff - Pat DuVal
The Early Troubles - Gerard Rose
The Boy Captain - Gerard Rose
Bless Me Father - Gerard Rose
For I Have Sinned - Gerard Rose
A Western Hero - Gerard Rose
Red Smith in LA Noir - David Jones
The Shadow Candidate - Rich Robinson
Hustle is Heaven - Duncan Matteson
Vision for a Healthy California - Bill Monning
Three Lives of a Warrior - Phil Butler
Live Better Longer - Hugh Wilson
Green-Lighting Your Future / How You Can
 Manifest the Perfect Life - John Koeberer

www.ingramcontent.com/pod-product-compliance
Lightning Source LLC
Chambersburg PA
CBHW072231170626
46813CB00003B/1177